E Clairmonte

The Africander; A Plain Tale of Colonial Life

E Clairmonte

The Africander; A Plain Tale of Colonial Life

ISBN/EAN: 9783744751650

Printed in Europe, USA, Canada, Australia, Japan

Cover: Foto ©Andreas Hilbeck / pixelio.de

More available books at **www.hansebooks.com**

THE AFRICANDER

A Plain Tale of Colonial Life

BY

E. CLAIRMONTE

ILLUSTRATED

LONDON

T. FISHER UNWIN

PATERNOSTER SQUARE

1896

LIST OF ILLUSTRATIONS

THE AFRICANDER.

CHAPTER I.

THE following narrative has no pretensions to be more than a simple record of diverse aspects of life in South Africa.

It has no claim to literary style—not even to chosen terms; it is rather a plain, unvarnished setting down of facts that may prove of interest and of use to all such as either contemplate going out there in search of living or in quest of adventure, or merely taking interest in it as the "land of promise" of the immediate future.

Some time in the year 1877 I started for South Africa, a callow lad of fourteen. I had left it a mere child.

A

Landing at Port Elizabeth, I found a Cape cart with a Hottentot driver waiting; he had been sent to meet me from the ostrich farm to where I was bound, a distance of 250 miles. We had a hot weary drive, over hot dusty roads, fringed with mimosa and prickly pear bushes; at times we were almost deafened by the shrill persistent note of the grasshopper; now and then a steinbok or *duyker* would dash along to what he deemed a safe point of vantage, where he would stand fixedly, and gaze sideways at us until we were lost to view. The clucking of a guinea-fowl might be heard in accompaniment to the queer note of the *kook-a-vic*, and a flock of long-tailed mousebirds, called *finks*, would dash past to settle in a *rooihout* tree, erecting their crests like cockatoes, and screaming at us in indignant protest.

But it was pleasant in the sweet, cool evenings to drive through the mimosa-

A SOUTH AFRICAN DRIVE ON ROAD TO FARM.

scented air, and listen to the strange noises of the many different insects, animals, and birds. When our road happened to wind under high cliffs, we could hear the loud, hoarse "baugh—m, baugh—m, baugh-—m!" of the baboons. A sentinel keeping watch and ward for his companions, busy gathering roots and succulent plants amongst the rocks, would call a warning at our approach, and, on looking up, we could see dozens of them scamper up the hill, barking "baugh—m, baugh—m," in their insolent way. Far over-head blue cranes uttering their cracked note as they flew; and the lively *sprew*, darting amongst the bushes with dark-brown back and yellow belly, and piping song; and the ring-necked doves cooing their love in the trees—all helped to make the long drive less wearisome. The sunsets, too—the beautiful Cape sunsets—amongst the mountains were most lovely. One moment hidden by a peak we would watch the rich

play of its light and shade on the mountains'
rugged sides, then passing round a point we
could see the blood-red globe just disappearing over the horizon, leaving the clouds
behind it stained with ever-changeful hues.
Sometimes our road brought us past fields
of "mealies," waving their plumes over the
young ears of corn, or flocks of fat-tailed
sheep feeding on the rich grass pasture.
Then the low thatched roof of the farm
homestead would appear: the building
itself surrounded by a *stoep* (verandah),
with a glass door opening on to it from
each room; at a little distance from the
back of the house the *kraals*, made of thorn
bushes, into which the stock are driven at
night and counted; and still a little further
off the cone-shaped huts in which the Kaffir
and Hottentot servants sleep, lying like a
cluster of bee-hives. In front of the house
the "lands" (fields) stretch away in the
distance, and the immediate foreground is

generally filled by an orange grove, or a quaint old garden rich in flowers and fruit. Although totally unlike in character, a nice Cape farm homestead is quite as attractive in its way as a typical English one. The inns we stopped at were all clean and comfortable. The few Colonials in them, drinking "Cape smoke," were quiet and gentlemanly, without any of the swagger and bluster one finds in other countries. The Cape Colonist is a gentleman born and bred of the best stock : he is generally genial and open-hearted, with plenty of sound common sense ; and, as rider and the most deadly shot, perhaps not to be matched in the world ; in other words, good all-round man and sportsman.

My driver smoked and chewed alternately strong Cape tobacco, which had for me then a most repulsive smell ; indeed he did not smell very nice himself, especially in the hotter part of the day. Later on I got used to the tobacco of the country, and soon preferred it to any other, as is the case with most who try it. After a while "Cape smoke" (Colonial brandy) even becomes palatable, more especially in parts where liquor of any sort is scarce. Cape sherry and Pontac (port) are excellent wines when at their best. The best tobacco is grown in the Transvaal, and is more expensive than that of the Cape. Quantities of the latter is sold as low as sixpence a pound, and is largely used as sheep-dressing in cases of scab, called there *brandtseikte;* and a weekly allowance of a "span" is given to each farm hand. It is wonderful how the quality of tobacco varies from the different soil in which it is grown. Great care and a large amount of labour is needed to produce it, and no crop impoverishes the soil so much. A short description may be of interest to some readers.

Firstly, a seed bed is prepared of a mixture of fine mould, sand, and wood ashes, then the seeds are sown and barely covered. The land for the reception of the seedlings is heavily manured, ploughed, and repeatedly harrowed. When in a highly pulverised state it is finally ploughed into furrows two feet apart, and cross-ploughed at the same distance ; this leaves equal squares, in all two feet apart. The seedlings are then pulled and carried on litters by two men ; another man receives them, and places one on each square ; he, in turn, is followed by another hand who dibbles one into each square. After this, men are constantly kept hoeing, irrigating, and picking off caterpillars —the greatest pest of the tobacco-grower. As soon as buds have formed, the plant is immediately " topped "; a shoot springs from the base of each leaf; these all require to be picked off to keep the strength in the main leaves. The moment the colour begins to change, the plant is lopped and allowed to wilt. Great experience is necessary to know the exact time to lop. When duly wilted, the plants are collected in carts or litters, and carried to the drying sheds, and spread on tables. Men are then employed in threading the butt of the plants on long thin sticks, which are then attached to the beams and sides of the building, allowing the plants to hang. When quite dry, the leaves are so brittle that it is impossible to handle them without breaking; so a moist day is chosen, then the leaves are stripped off the stems and sorted into three qualities—tops, middles, and bottoms, or ground leaves, the latter being the inferior sort. They are then tied into " hands," that is, a number of leaves placed on top of each other, and tied at the shanks. These " hands " are then laid in large heaps on the floor, and well covered with blankets for sweating. It needs further judgment to tell when the sweating process has gone far enough; this is gauged by putting one's hand in and judging the heat. When hot enough, the heap is scattered, cooled, and re-sweated, this process being continued until all the natural moisture is absorbed, and no further sweating possible.

Of course there are many improvements on this rough and ready process on larger tobacco-growing farms since my time, but, nevertheless, this method is still pursued in many places.

Crossing the Baviaan River, we passed out of the grass country into the vast Karroo. Here the total aspect of the scene is changed. No grass whatever is to be seen, except on a close examination, when a few small scattered tufts may be discerned. Trees are less plentiful ; only a few varieties grow on the banks of the rivers, the thorny mimosa being the most numerous. The overhanging *krantze* are covered with aloes, prickly pear, wild coffee, and *spekboem* bushes. Lizards of various size and hue lie basking in the sun ; perhaps a black-brown tortoise will crawl slowly between the bushes and gaze at you with sleepy black eyes ; go closer, and watch how quickly he will draw in his snake-like head and little round stumpy feet. Walk to the mimosa-trees that fringe the river bank, and you will see the pear-shaped nests of the finks, with little holes for entrance as in our kitty-wrens, hanging over the water from the branches of the wild tobacco-tree. Here, too, you will find the larder of the "butcher" bird—large flies, butter-flies, and beetles of many colours impaled on thorns. The brilliant-plumaged " sugar " or honey birds are darting about with their long, curved bills. Although you are pick-ing your way carefully, you will suddenly find yourself entangled in a " wait-a-bit " bush, the sharp, curved, fish-hook-like thorns of which will coerce you to " wait a while " to free your-self. From a tree across the river a grey monkey will peer at you, but as soon as he sees he is observed, he is off to a hiding-place with his companions. You come to some reeds growing thickly next the bank, and hear a splash ; stand a while and you will see the head of a *logavaan* or iguana rise to the surface after his dive, swim rapidly to the opposite bank, and disappear. Two storks, each standing on one leg in the shallows, gazing mournfully at the water, rise in alarm and fly off, uttering their discordant, rasping cry. Now and then you may be startled by a crash in some adjacent bushes; there is no cause for alarm ; it is only a duyker disturbed from his siesta. The many birds with their strange calls are interesting, and you will not fail to note the absence of song among the South African birds.

The country we were passing through was fresh and green after the late rains. People told me that they had just had a bad drought, no rain had fallen through many months of scorching hot weather. Droughts affect the

grass country much more than the Karroo,
and the farmers in the former generally *trek*
away with their stock in the dry seasons to
districts where pasture can be found.   In the
Karroo it is different.   The little heath- and
thyme-like bushes stand the dry weather
much better.   When rain does come, the
change is instantaneous, almost magical.
The whole country is clothed in vivid green,
and the little bushes are quickly covered
with sweet-scented flowers of every colour ;
animal as well as vegetable life seems to
assume an aspect of freshness and gaiety.

On we pushed, the good roan ponies feeling none the worse for their journey, and at
last we arrived at a white farmhouse, on the
bank of the Great Fish River, a few miles
from the pretty little town of Cradock.   It
was getting dusk, and I was tired, and sat
down with appetite to a supper of venison
and boiled green mealies, content to have
arrived at my destination.

CHAPTER II.

THE next morning I went for a walk with
Smith, who was the *klein-baas* of the farm.
Klein-baas is the term used for the sub-
manager, and "baas" is the manager or proprietor. Taking guns with us, we walked
through some mealie fields towards the river,
where he expected to get a bok of some
sort. On the way we passed several paddocks
where breeding pairs of ostriches were kept.
On seeing us the old cock bird would stalk
grandly up with tail and head erect—lashing
his wings with rage, and follow us as far as
his fence would permit. Then he would
squat down, and fluttering his wings, rock
himself from side to side, thumping his curved

neck on his back. This they always do, not only to people, but to their hens in the breeding season. Close to the river Smith shot a steinbok; the shot roused his mate, at which I fired and missed—excusable, perhaps, as it was my first shot. On the way back I practised at birds, feeling more at home after every attempt. Breakfast over, we mounted ponies and rode round the farm and saw the stock, and my duties were pointed out to me. I was allowed a week's holiday. Smith was glad of a companion, and often accompanied me on short shooting expeditions, as I was ambitious to improve. I had many shots at springbok, duyker, and steinbok, but rarely hit any. One night we arranged a porcupine hunt, with the off chance of getting an antbear. We had invited two or three neighbours to sup and go with us. We had armed ourselves with spears, and mounting our ponies, started off with half a dozen dogs. We spread out in skirmishing order, the dogs searching ahead, and rode silently across the plain. Before long, barking, snapping, snarling, and a loud howl of pain reached our ears, and galloping forward we came upon the scene. A fine porcupine was standing at bay in the moonlight, with its quills erect, and as the dogs dashed at it, they received severe wounds from the sharp quills. Dismounting to save our horses' legs, we quickly despatched it, and went on searching for another, which we were lucky enough to find. On our way home we killed an antbear, and found it an even more difficult customer to tackle, on account of the toughness of its skin and its activity. These animals are not killed for their meat, which, by the way, is held in esteem by the natives, but because they are such destructive creatures—the porcupine destroying crops of mealies and pumpkins; the antbear burrowing holes about the veldt, which makes riding dangerous, and causes horses and ostriches running loose

B

at night to get their legs broken. The
monkeys are also a nuisance. They are very
fond of pumpkins, and we tried several ways
of catching them. One method was by
constructing a large trap cage, with branches
and leaves to make it look natural, and
fixing it in the bush; the heavy lid of
which is held open by means of a lever
fastened to the top of it. One end of this
lever tends a short distance behind the
cage; to this end a short stick is attached,
with a notch cut in the end of it, which hangs
down above another short stick that is slipped
through the back of the cage for the purpose of holding the bait. The cover is then
opened, and the notch stick drops on to the
bait stick. A piece of pumpkin is fastened
to the end which is in the cage, and the trap
is complete. The monkey catching hold of
the pumpkin causes the notch stick to slip
off the bait stick, and the cover falls to,
making him a prisoner. Another more

simple method, and rather an amusing one, is this. The monkeys are very fond of pumpkin seeds, so a pumpkin with a small hole cut in it is placed near their haunt. The monkey slips his hand in easily enough, grabs a good fistful of seeds, and tries to withdraw them. The hole is not big enough for the passage of his clenched hand, and he has not sense enough to reason this out; so whilst he is struggling with the pumpkin it is easy to settle him by a rap on the head with a *knob-kerrie*.

Riding out one day with Smith to collect some ostriches, we noticed a little brown bird, which kept chirping and flitting around us. Smith at once recognised it as the honey-bird, and said that, if we were to follow it, it would lead us to a bees' nest. We reined in our horses, and the little bird took a short flight in one direction, and back to us again. After it had repeated this manœuvre several times, we proceeded to follow it; it led us up a *kloof*, and there, sure enough in the hollow trunk of a *spekboem* trèe, was a fine bees' nest. We smoked out the bees, and turning our soft felt hats inside out, put in the combs, and cantered home with them, not forgetting, however, to leave some for our little feathered guide. This little bird is known to take leopards, baboons, and other animals to bees' nests, and it is said that not only do thè animals know the object of the bird, but they always leave it some honey, or allow it to eat with them !

One morning at breakfast we were disturbed by a Kaffir herd, who ran in, calling out : " The baboons are stealing eggs." Up we jumped, seized our rifles from the gun-rack, and ran down towards the ostrich camps. One side of the breeding birds' paddocks was bounded by the river, and the baboons had crossed it from the rocky hill on the opposite side. So Mr Barker, the baas, who was a crack shot, crossed over

BABOON KRANTZ.

to intercept them, whilst we prepared to tackle them on our side. As usual, there was one keeping watch, and as soon as he caught sight of us, he gave the alarm, and off they scampered in the direction of Mr Barker, who was hiding in some bushes.

We fired a few shots without any effect, and paused to watch the sport on the other side. The baboons, thinking they were safe, began to "baugh—m," and their loud bark echoed down the hillside. Presently a white puff of smoke rolled out of some bushes amongst the rocks, and we saw a large baboon tumble down the hillside. Another puff, another, and the whole troop scampered up the steep hill at a wonderful pace, to disappear over the brow. Going home to finish our breakfast, we could hear their "baughing" behind us, as if in derision at our attempt to shoot them. Mr Barker soon arrived with a Kaffir carrying the dead baboon, which was skinned to make whip lashes for the stock whips.

These raids were becoming a great nuisance as well as a serious loss, for they destroyed quantities of ostrich eggs, which, at that time, were valued at five pounds each. We planned to hunt them the next day, with the assistance of our neighbours, who were also troubled by them. Messages were sent round, and next morning twelve of us breakfasted together, and started with a dozen dogs to scour the hills. They are such wary brutes that it takes considerable strategy to get near them.

Having lost one pack, we surrounded another hill, and, with the help of the dogs, succeeded in keeping them on the top. The dogs were amongst them before we arrived, and we could hear a fierce fight above us. Scrambling up as fast as we could, we came right into the thick of it. One dog lay dead, and several were bleeding badly from severe wounds. We killed most of them before they could escape; the dogs had not killed

one. It would take a very large and powerful dog to master a baboon, and, in any case,
he would stand a poor chance. These fellows
stand about four feet high, with powerful
jaws, and arms that hang nearly to their feet.
One of them would catch a small dog in its
strong grip, and meeting its teeth in a
fleshy part, rip the unfortunate animal to
pieces, and throw it aside. A Cape dog is
strong, and very game, and will nearly
always kill a snake when he meets one.
We had another skirmish with a small troop,
with good results, and went home satisfied
that we would be left in peace for a time.

Baboon-killing is, to me, too unpleasant
to be called sport. The resemblance to
humanity, though unflattering, is too close.
They are the only animals I know that meet
one with a look in their eyes of positive intelligent human expression; and once when
a female baboon I had shot put her little
black finger in the wound and drew it out, red

with blood, showing it to me with a piteous look in her eyes, and a cry like a hurt child, it made me quite sick, and I felt a kind of pang of conscience.

Another great pest, and a curious one, is the bird we call the white-necked crow. This bird, which is much larger than the common crow, picks up a stone in its claws, and breaks the ostrich eggs by dropping it on to them from a considerable height. It then flies down and devours the egg. I have known it to drive the sitting bird off its nest by the same method, to enable it to drop a stone on the eggs. Whenever one was seen about, we used to hide in bushes near the nest, and now and then succeeded in shooting one.

An ostrich farmer is hampered by many drawbacks. The birds are continually getting their legs broken in fences and holes; sometimes, indeed, they manage to break their necks. Ostriches are said to have the smallest quantity of brains of any known bird in proportion to their size. They are, indeed, signally stupid; for instance, some mealies had dropped from a bag at feeding-time, outside a gate leading to a breeding paddock. The hen-bird, seeing these, thrust her head through and ate them. In pulling her neck back again, her head caught in an angle in the gate. By simply lowering it, she could have passed it through easily, but, instead of doing that, she tugged and tugged until she lay sprawling on her back minus her head. On another occasion I was trying to drive a bird across a railway line that was not fenced in, but the obstinate brute refused to go over, and gave me half an hour's hard galloping. Finally, a train dashed up, and I then endeavoured to drive the bird away from the line; but no, he then decided to cross over. The train reached us, and the stupid thing raced alongside of the engine, trying to get round it, I galloping with it. I shouted to the engine-driver to put steam on, as the whistle had been blown to no purpose. The side of the train was lined with passengers' heads enjoying the scene. The driver then let steam out of the lower valves ; this playing upon the ostrich's legs scared him, and, with a frantic jump aside, he rolled down the enbankment, fortunately not injuring himself. Though on a smart horse, I was left some distance behind, which proves how fast an ostrich can go, although I'd back a horse against one in a five-mile race.

CHAPTER III.

ONE day we shot over the mountains at the back of the farm. They ran almost in a semicircle—the side sloping up to a krantz about thirty feet high ; above this a wide plateau stretched, where a few rheabok and some thirty quagga ran. We never allowed anyone to shoot the quagga, as they were said to be the only ones left south of latitude 28° ; moreover, we had an idea of catching the young ones some day, and breaking them in. This is sometimes done with success. They are very similar in marking to the zebra, are of smaller build, very low in the withers, and with the endurance of the mule. The evening before, a shepherd had run in, in a great state of alarm, to say that a large *ingive* (leopard) had killed six sheep. It had gone off with the carcass of one. We tracked it for nearly a mile, only to find a few bones left. Thinking it would return to the others it had killed, we kept watch all night, but saw no sign of it, so we started with about a dozen beaters to shoot over the mountain, where some of these beasts had their lair. We ranged ourselves in a long line on the plateau, whilst the beaters spread out in another, down the sloping side, calling in Kaffir to the leopard : " Come out! you are wanted. You are only a frightened dog!" or any other insulting remark that might occur to them. The ground they were beating was dotted thickly over with small bushes, and great numbers of a small antelope, called *grysbok*, were driven out before the beaters. We fired down upon these as they darted amongst the bushes, the heavy firing echoing down the mountain

sides. The beaters picked them up as fast
as they were shot, and by six o'clock, when
we had reached the other end of the mountain, twenty-two of these bok had been
dropped, but not a trace of a leopard had
been found. I discovered the next day I
had left my silver flask on the top at
luncheon time, so I rode up to get it. I
saw a quagga stallion up there, and gave
chase to see how fast he could go. I gained
on him rapidly until we reached some stony
ground, and then he got away from me. I
was not, however, mounted on a very good
horse.

The average Colonial horses are not handsome ; they are rather low in the withers,
slightly cowhocked, and straight in the
shoulder. They are, however, noted for their
wonderful endurance ; they will keep up a
hard gallop for many miles without tiring,
and to ride one a hundred miles in a day is
a common occurrence. The Colonials rarely

trot their horses ; they either canter or amble. A fast amble is called a "tripple," a word that expresses the pace admirably.

Ostrich-farming at that time was paying wonderfully well ; farmers were selling out sheep and other stock in order to invest in it. The high price of feathers, however, was bound not to last long. It is still carried on, but not to such a great extent.

In 1877 a breeding pair of birds, five or six years old, would fetch up to £300, and best prime feathers as high as £80 per lb. In 1884 £100 was considered a good price for similar birds, and £40 per lb. for the same class of feather.

The ostrich is a bird indigenous to Africa, being found in most parts of this continent. It belongs to the same family as the emu, the rhea, or South American ostrich, and the cassowary, but differs from these in the following particulars: first, by having only two toes ; secondly, by the head and neck being bare of feathers ; thirdly, by being twice the size of any of the others, and its eggs averaging upwards of three pounds in weight ; fourthly, by the beauty of its plumage, the feathers of the others being of little commercial value ; fifthly, by the male and female differing in colour, the male ostrich being black and the female grey.

The ostrich differs from most other birds by its wings being unadapted for flight, and the barb of the feather being of equal length on each side of the quill. The age to which an ostrich can live is matter of conjecture—possibly to one hundred years ; but we never knew of one dying from old age. It was in the year 1867 that the first attempt at keeping ostriches in a state of domestication, and breeding from them, was made at the Cape. Before that period the birds ran wild, and were hunted and killed for their feathers.

The originators of ostrich-farming received but little encouragement at first. Most people thought it was a ridiculous idea to attempt to farm a bird of so timid a nature, or to expect they would breed in confinement, or that the progeny could ever be yarded, handled, or driven in mobs like other stock. It was asserted also that the feathers from tame birds would not curl ; this was even believed by feather dealers, and for some time a strong prejudice prevailed against the feathers of such. Success however attended the attempt to domesticate the birds; they laid eggs, hatched them, and it was found that the young ostriches could be reared as tamely as barn-door fowls. People began to see that a new industry was being established which was decidedly a money-making one; forthwith a rage sprang up for ostriches, and the industry spread so that in a few years there were few parts of the Cape Colony where ostriches in state of domestication were not to be seen. The value of feathers exported from the Cape in 1867 was £70,000, these being all from

OSTRICHES.

wild birds.   The export for 1880, £888,632,
principally tame birds' feathers ; and it was estimated at this time that a capital of £8,000,000
was invested in the industry.   For a number
of years ostrich-farming was confined to the
Cape Colony, with the exception of an attempt
of the French to establish it at Algiers ; later
on, people in other countries began to turn
their attention to the ostrich, and a number
of birds were taken to North and South
America, India, and Australia.   The Cape
farmers became alarmed at the prospect of so
much competition from other countries, and
a bill was introduced and passed by the Cape
Parliament imposing an export duty of £100 on
each ostrich exported from the Cape Colony,
and £5 on each ostrich egg.   A few days
after the passing of the Act, an American
gentleman arrived, prepared to purchase and
take away 300 birds, but the sum of £30,000
required by the Customs deterred him from
carrying his project into effect.

The pasture of South Africa is particularly well adapted for ostriches, and it is only on well-stocked farms that they require to be fed. Mealies and chopped prickly-pear leaves form the staple food.

Our farm consisted of 600 *morgen*, which is about equivalent to 1200 English acres, and we generally had 700 birds running on it. This included fourteen pairs of breeding birds, each pair in a separate paddock of two or three acres.

The ostrich reaches maturity in three or four years. The cock bird is then very savage, and a kick from him will sometimes kill a man. A long thorny branch, called a " tock," is held against the sensitive neck of a bird to prevent him attacking. Three-year-olds will sometimes breed, but it is not advisable to let them, as a weakly progeny is generally the result. In selecting ostriches for breeding, we chose those with long white feathers and good muscular development. In paddocks of the above extent they will lay and hatch out chicks on an allowance of mealies of only a pound each a day. They generally lay from twelve to eighteen eggs in a nest, scratched in the soil by their powerful feet. Both assist at this work by scooping the earth out backwards. The hen generally sits during the day, the cock taking her place on the nest shortly before sundown, and remaining there until about nine o'clock the next morning. He then guards the nest jealously, and woe betide the man who ventures near without a "tock." I once received a kick which laid me up for a fortnight.

The incubation occupies forty-two days; the chicks are left with their parents for a fortnight, then caught, taken charge of by a herd, who chops up green food and bones for them. At five months old they are herded like cattle on the veldt.

An incubator is an article that cannot well be dispensed with by a breeder of ostriches ; as sometimes, particularly with young breeding birds, the cock will refuse to sit, and if no incubator be at hand, the nest of eggs will be useless : besides, too, during severe weather, such as hail and thunder storms, sitting birds may leave their nest and refuse to take to them again ; in such a case, if the eggs are removed to the incubator before they get cold, the chicks will hatch out. By the use of this machine a larger number of chicks can be reared if the eggs are taken away as fast as they are laid, and five or six imitations are left in their place ; if this is done, they will lay as many as thirty or forty eggs without stopping, whereas, if the eggs are left in the nest, they will only lay from twelve to eighteen, and then commence sitting. It is not advisable to force the birds to lay too much in this manner, or weak birds will be the result ; a far better plan is to let the birds sit on the eggs for fourteen days, and then remove them to the incubator.

This prevents the birds from being brought into low condition by long sitting, and they will soon have another nest. The proper temperature for the eggs is 100° for 36 days, then it is lowered to 98° until the chicks are hatched out. The eggs are turned in the drawers twice daily ; a day or two before the hatching the chick will be seen to fall in the shell, the air-space being thereby considerably enlarged. This can be observed by holding the egg against the light, and shading the end of the egg with the hand ; it soon begins to rise again until the egg is quite full ; at this stage it should be marked, and if in twenty-four hours the chick has not yet broken through, the shell should be cracked and a piece of it chipped off at the air-space ; this done, the chick could extricate itself without further assistance. It is exceedingly interesting to watch the nicety with which the ostrich will perform this operation. Selecting an egg in which it knows there is a chick unable to break through, it will roll it gently over with its beak until it is in the proper position under the hard horny substance of the bird's breast, where sufficient force to break the shell without injuring the chick can be applied. The chicks are fed by hand with cut lucerne, bran mashes, and any chopped vegetables, until they are four months old ; after that they are herded as the older ones.

The age of birds can be determined as follows : At seven months old, the first crop of feathers are quite ripe ; that is, the drab feathers can be pulled out without causing bleeding, and the long whiter quill feathers can be cut. At twelve months old the second growth of feathers will be well forward, and some of the cocks begin to get their black plumage, and show white on the front of their legs and along the edge of their beaks. At two years old the cocks will be quite black, none of the narrow, pointed chicken feathers being visible, except where the neck joins the body; the hens will in like manner have lost all their chicken feathers, which will be replaced by drabs.

Three years old—at this age the plumage has reached perfection; the cocks show pink on the front of their legs and beak, and no trace of chicken feathers is discernible. At four years they have reached maturity, and no further guide to their age is possible.

They are marked in various ways. Some owners file notches in their long toes, others paint a patch of paint on their necks or legs, but most farmers brand their initials on the bird's thigh.

In the early days of ostrich farming at the Cape, it was usual to pluck the feathers every six months; but it was soon found that by this practice the birds were rendered of little value in a few years, the feathers at each succeeding plucking becoming shorter and stiffer until useless. The feathers are at

their best after six months' growth, and in
the case of quill feathers or long white ones,
if left on the birds for even a week longer,
begin to deteriorate ; the tips become worn,
and this, of course, detracts much from the
value of the feather. After six months'
growth, the blood vein in the quill has dried
up to the point where it enters the wing,
and the feather can be cut close to the wing
without drawing blood or giving pain to the
bird. It is this plan of cutting the quill
feathers which is now generally adopted.
The short feathers—the blacks of the male
and drabs of the female—are pulled after
having eight months' growth, and are consequently quite dry ; pulling them does not
injure the bird in any way, and they are not
damaged as are the quill feathers by being
left so much longer. When the quill feathers
are cut, the blacks or drabs, as the case may
be, are pulled out ; the stumps of the quill
feathers are extracted in two months' time,

and in six months another plucking of feathers is ready. The short feathers have now eight months' growth, and the quills six; a full plucking being thus obtained from each bird every eight months. A strong pair of pruning shears is the best implement for cutting the feathers; a pair of small pincers is used for extracting the quill stumps.

A plucking yard is required for the taking of the feathers. This must be erected in such a way that access can be had to it from all the paddocks where the birds are running. The best kind of yard is constructed as follows :—Fence in an enclosure of about half an acre with a strong five-wire fence, the wires being interlaced with branches, and a wide gateway made for entrance of birds. At one corner of the enclosure put up a small yard about 12 + 18 feet, made of posts, with strong planks nailed across them, boarding it up to a height of five feet; at one end leave a wide gateway to admit the birds being driven in from the larger enclosure, and at the other end a door opening outwards, for passing the birds out after the plucking. Opposite this door erect inside the yard a box two feet wide, three deep, and four long, for the bird to stand in during the operation. The above arrangement gives the persons taking the feathers a better chance of doing their work properly, as the bird has no room to move about and struggle. It is quite necessary to have a long narrow bag to pull over the bird's head ; with this on, the wildest bird will generally stand perfectly still. When the time for plucking arrives, the mob are driven into the large enclosure, and from there into the smaller yard, where the bird is seized, blindfolded by the cap, and pushed into the box, plucked, entered on the tally-sheet, and let out to meditate on the wonderful change in his appearance, which has been effected in a few minutes.

There is no fixed time of the year for taking the feathers, and where a large number of birds are kept, and young ones are constantly being hatched, there will be feathers ready to be taken almost every month through the year. After the plucking of the birds is completed, the next operation will be sorting the feathers into the different classes and qualities, and packing for the London market. The sorter sits at a long table and sorts into heaps—"primes," "firsts," "seconds," "thirds," and "damaged."

CHAPTER IV.

I HAD worked hard for two years and learned every branch of Cape farming. Smith had left, and I had become *Klien-baas*, but I had not received any pay for my services. Beginners do not as a rule get any salary for the first year; they are taught farming, and sometimes have to pay as much as £120 a year for the privilege of learning. I was determined to try elsewhere, and sent many applications to other farmers, but did not succeed in getting a post. I was not contented, and had no interest in the welfare of the farm, as whatever happened I lost nothing and gained nothing. Besides, too, I had, with the rash impetuosity of youth, become engaged, and was anxious to make a definite position for myself. My *fiancé* lived in an old-fashioned house, surrounded with fig-trees, in the principal street of Cradock. This was, as in many other South African towns, lined on each side with fine mulberry-trees, the shedding of the soft ripe fruit of which is no little source of trouble to ladies in white gowns who may happen to walk under them.

Making up my mind to set out and look for work, I told Mr Barker of my intention. He was very angry, and we unfortunately had words. The next day I sold out all I possessed except a horse, saddle, and bridle, and started up country, stopping a week at a farm fifty miles away, belonging to a brother of Mr Barker. There the country was almost treeless; vast plains of Karroo stretching as far as the eye could reach, vanishing at the horizon, and giving an impression of intense solitude. Here and there the red brick farmhouse of some Dutchman might be

D

met, close to it a dam, the reddish water of which supplied the indwellers and animals alike. I was often obliged to halt at these houses for rest and food, and always found the people hospitable, and exceedingly tiresome.

On entering, the first word would be " *Affsaal?* " Then the fat *vrau* would step forward, holding out her big soft hand, the entire family, and anyone else who might be there, following suit. There is an odd lack of heartiness about a Boer's hand-shake; it is just a limp touch, very unlike an honest English grip. Weak coffee would then be handed round; this, by the way, they drink all day. This proceeding was always followed by an exchange of tobacco pouches and the never-varying questions as to where I was bound, from whence I had come; the weather is hot, cold, or dry, as the case may be. The ground once broken, they would entertain me with not a few lies as to the extent of their stock, or boasts of their shooting. At eight o'clock prayers and psalms for an hour, and then to bed. The latter is generally a home-made affair of wooden framework, called a "kartel." Strips of raw hide are stripped across for the support of an enormous feather-bed ; it is not at all uncommon for the whole household, regardless of age, sex, and relationship, to share the bed in common. The floors of the rooms are generally plastered with cow-dung ; this one does get used to, as it is not objectionable when dry. The best room is often smeared with coats of bullock's blood, until it looks and shines like ebony.

At the time at which I write, the country was suffering from a severe drought. The house at which I was staying was situated on a flat, monotonous, red plain. The dry, hard, brackish earth was covered with short, leafless Karroo bushes, small *kopjes* of red brown iron-stone dotting it here and there.

The leaves of the prickly pear had turned
from a brilliant green to a sickly blue, and
almost all the dams had dried into dirty red-
brown pools. The sheep staggered about,
fainting from weakness and starvation, unable
when down to rise to their feet again ; cattle
wandered about unsteadily, moaning for want
of food, whilst the pitiless sun poured down
its scorching rays from a glaring white sky.
The only green things visible were the milk
bushes—an *euphorbia* of a poisonous nature
—that grew like long thin fingers pointing
to the cloudless sky. The scene made an
indelible impression upon me. I seemed to
have arrived at " the land of desolation," and
I made up my mind to push on northwards.
However, my new friend advised me to go
south, and try my luck in British Kaffraria.
I was obliged to wait a week longer, as my
horse had become miserably thin ; the poor
fellow would come and almost beg for food.
I was obliged to feed him as best I could on

scraps of bread, a handful of mealies, or a few green weeds out of the scanty garden that was kept going from a well. There were plenty of springbok about, but too thin to be worth shooting.

At last I started on my way back from this land of drought. Avoiding the inns to save expense, I camped out at night under a bush, and hobbled my horse, giving him a bundle of forage, obtained at an inn sometime during the day. A horse's usual feed at the Cape consists of a sheaf of oats, cut into three-inch pieces by fixing a reaping-hook in a hole in the manger. My own lunch was a piece of bread and *billong* (dried beef or venison).

It was refreshing on reaching Cradock to see the green trees and the mountains once more. I called on Mabel, and told her of my altered plans, and heard that a friend of mine had obtained my last post at Mr Barker's. Leaving the next day, I rode sixty miles, passed through the pretty little town of Bedford, on the Kagha River, and reached Adelaide on the Koonap, where I stayed a week with some relations who owned a small farm.

There was no game to hunt here, so I amused myself walking down the river, shooting *logavaans* with a small rifle. They are useless, except for the sake of a lump of fat which is found inside them, and which makes the best oil in the world for cleaning firearms.

Whilst here, the startling news came of the breaking out of the Zulu War, and filled me with the idea of offering myself as a volunteer. The next day on my journey I resolved to sell my horse at East London, go up to Natal by a coasting steamer, and join the forces. What did it matter what I undertook? I was young and strong, with five pounds in my pocket, besides having a horse and rifle. I felt as

lighthearted as any adventurer of olden tale,
and, no doubt, had a devil-may-care way of
taking the vicissitudes of life.

Sleeping at Alice that night, I arrived
at King William's Town the next day, and
put up at a hotel. Seeing a poster with a
notice of a sale of horses to be held the following day, I rode up with mine, and requested
the auctioneer to sell it with saddle and bridle
just as it stood. It was knocked down for
£20 to a Major H——, who put to me
some questions concerning it. Having informed him of the horse's good qualities, and
the distance I had ridden him, we got into
conversation. He had only arrived a few
days before from Natal for the purpose of
buying horses for the remounts ; he required a
hundred and twenty to take to Natal overland.

Here was my chance. He was an Englishman, only stationed a year in Natal, not
used to Cape travelling, and unable to speak
any of the native languages.

We had arranged to meet again the next day, so I determined to offer him my assistance, did so, and it was accepted willingly. He took me to the Government Compounds, where I saw some fifty horses he had bought ; he had certainly given good prices for them, and declared that bargaining through an interpreter was not satisfactory.

He had put advertisements in the local papers, notifying he was open to buy mounts, and dealers and farmers were bringing in horses every day. Remaining at the Compound all day, we examined a good many and bought a few. When he found that a horse was suitable, he left it for me to buy, which I did to his satisfaction. He asked me to dine with him that night, and after dinner I mentioned my desire to go to the front. He promised to aid me with all his power, and telegraphed the next morning for permission to employ me to assist him on the journey with the horses. The request was

granted in a few days' time in a despatch
that also fixed my salary at 16s. 6d.
a day. He congratulated me heartily, and
I thanked him in like terms. My satisfaction at earning money for the first time
in my life was great. I was soon rigged
out in a plain undress uniform, and the
days passed pleasantly until we had made up
the full complement of horses. This done,
we started on our long journey. Our route
lay through Komgha, the Transkei, Tembu-
land and Pondoland, a distance of about
450 miles.

The journey was rather uneventful. The
country through which we passed was most
beautiful. Sometimes we rode through
a perfect forest of tambookie grass, that
waved in places above the horses' heads, or
threaded our way through deep gorges, swam
rivers, and climbed mountains.

We had sixteen bastard Hottentot drivers,
besides two who acted as servants and

led the pack-horses. These fellows make capital grooms, but are unmitigated scoundrels otherwise. At this time a good many of them were used as jockeys, and rode some of the best horses; the only trouble they gave was the occasional need of a good thrashing.

The finest country we passed through was, I think, Pondoland. Never have I seen a land with such prospects in a general way— deep rich soil and splendid pastures, fairly well timbered with hard woods, intersected by picturesque valleys and numerous streams; its hills, reputed to hold great wealth in minerals, covered with waving grass.

Game is now scarce, but sport can be had with partridges and *pauw* (wild turkey), while the angler might find use for his rod in the many rivers that flow through the beautiful valleys. The valuable sea-cow (*du-gong*) is found in numbers in the Unzimkulu River, near the mouth of which there are

A PONDO,

facilities for making a good port. There seems no doubt that the best parts of South Africa are occupied by natives. Consider the vast Karroo in the Eastern Province, the Western Province, the Transvaal, and Orange Free State, and you will find none of them compare favourably with Pondoland, Zulu-land, or Zwaziland. The latter countries are not afflicted by the droughts, as are the former; indeed, if they were, the natives could not live as they do.

Their mode of cultivation is exceedingly primitive. The men do no work. They lie in a blanket in the sunshine, smoking, taking snuff, and drinking *tjwala* (Kaffir beer); they get up now and then for a feed of mealies and Kaffir-corn cakes. The women take hoes, stand in a line, and cross-hoe the fields, whilst other women follow and sow. That is the only cultivation the land gets, yet the crops are splendid. They grow mealies, Kaffir corn, and tobacco. The surplus mealies are sold, and the money spent in blankets, which are their only need—happy people!

The village consists of twenty to fifty huts, with three-feet high entrances. In the centre is the kraal into which the cattle belonging to the various families are driven in the evening. This done, the men slouch lazily in, and sit in the kraal to watch their *incomos* (cows), and talk; indeed, cattle is their favourite topic of conversation; the epic of the cow might be gleaned from their unwearying narratives. They do not care for cattle or sheep; a cow is their chief pride. With them they buy their wives and sell their daughters; they half live upon the milk, and the bull calves are killed and eaten. They have so little else in common with the world that it is small wonder they worship the cow.

When the winter is just over, and the long grass is dry, the men go out with old muzzle-loading guns, assagais, and *knobkerries,*

PONDO WOMEN.

and surround a few acres of ground, having set fire to the windward side of it. They rarely return without half a dozen buck and some birds. The latter are thrown on to the fire just as they are, until burnt pretty black, and then everything is eaten except the bill and legs. They are very expert in knocking over partridges and other birds by throwing sticks at them ; indeed, even a rabbit or hare has but little chance of escaping their un- erring aim. I often thought I would like to see some of them shy at an Aunt Sally at an English fair ; the proprietor's stock of cocoa- nuts would rapidly diminish.

One day, after a ride of twenty miles, we arrived at the bank of a river—the Umlaas, I think—which was in flood, and we thought it wiser policy to stay the night there rather than risk a crossing. We had during our journey crossed several rivers in flood, and experienced some difficulty in landing the horses on the opposite bank, some being

F

washed down half a mile. After we had seen the camp formed, the guards turned out with the horses, and the picketing ropes got ready, H—— and I took towels and strolled to the river to find a quiet place to bathe. It was running very swiftly; the water was yellowish in colour. We did not mind the colour, but the speed of the water amongst the huge boulders made bathing uncomfortable, so we wandered further down and found a quiet spot where the river had made inroads amongst some trees. Here the flood had made no perceptible difference. The water was still, the place looked dark and shut out from the sun. I did not like the look of it for some reason, and shuddered to think of plunging into the cold depths. One hears at times of people diving into these African rivers and never rising to the surface again. They probably get caught in fallen branches, or stuck in mud or quicksands.

However, we said nothing to each other of

our feelings on the matter, and commenced to undress quietly—I do not think I ever took off my clothes so slowly in all my life—and when I had divested myself of my last garment, I found that H—— had finished at exactly the same moment. I sat still as a mouse, gazing at the gloomy water, hoping that he would go in first; but he was equally bent on waiting for me. I then asked him why he did not go in; he suggested that I should have first go; this I emphatically declined. We finally decided to toss who should take the dreaded plunge. We did so, and I lost. H—— laughed loudly, and I remember his laugh struck me as uncanny in that weird place. I felt much inclined to propose looking for a fresh place, but did not like to appear afraid. I would ten times sooner have chanced a dive in the yellow water amidst the boulders. However, I went to the edge of the bank, poised for a dive, and had already let myself go when I saw a snake, about six feet in length, swimming along the surface of the water. There was no way of saving myself, and with a sort of involuntary yell I fell plump on to it, and felt it slither round my body. The water was icy cold and my feelings indescribable. I have no doubt the snake was quite as frightened as I was. I did not sink very deep, and scrambled out as quickly as possible. H—— had seen all, and when I climbed up the bank he was busy putting on his clothes, and there was an end to our bathing experiment.

CHAPTER V.

On the sixteenth day we arrived at Pieter-maritzburg, delivered the horses at the stables, and reported ourselves at head-quarters in Longmarket Street.

Pietermaritzburg is named after Pieter Maritz, a powerful Boer, who *trekked* north and founded the colony. It is the capital of Natal, and one of the prettiest towns in South Africa. Its streets are wide, and its bungalow - like houses nestle amongst every variety of tree. It has a population of about 18,000. The market square, which is the business centre of the town, is always alive with vehicles of every description, from the brick wagon, with its long team of oxen, to the Cape cart and American "spider," which is so much used throughout South Africa.

Coolies are very numerous in Natal. The majority of them are, perhaps, to be found in Durban, but here I saw numbers of them, in their cool white clothes and turbans, carrying baskets of fruit suspended from the ends of a bamboo over their shoulders. In the worst part of the town, many of them had shops, in which they sold goods imported from India adapted to their own needs.

The natives are made up of Bacas, Tongas, and Natal Zulus, who are not the pure breed. The police are natives, armed with a *knobkerrie*, and dressed in white.

The military element was very strong in the town at that date, and met one at every turn. English red-coats, cavalry, the picturesque uniform of the Natal Mounted Police and Border Rangers, rumbling gun-

ZULU POLICEMEN.

carriages, and heavy commissariat wagons gave a lively impression of the stirring events to come.

A week after our arrival I had an appointment at the War Office to receive my pay. I had asked Major H—— to put in a word in my favour at headquarters—to say I was anxious for an appointment at the front. He said I would prove useful in the Army Service Corps, and that he would recommend me. Walking up Longmarket Street, I saw the horses we had brought up already mounted by Baker's Horse, a nondescript volunteer corps raised hurriedly at Port Elizabeth. Their uniforms were yellow corduroy breeches and gaiters, soft yellow felt hats with a red puggaree; during the campaign they were dubbed "the Canaries." They were on their way to join the fighting column at Kambula, which was commanded by Col. Sir Evelyn Wood, V.C. I quite forget the name of the officer in charge when I called to hear my fate, but he was very cordial, mentioning that he had received excellent accounts of me, but had no idea I was so young. I was obliged to admit that I was barely seventeen. Anyhow he promised to mention me in some despatches he was forwarding to General Strickland, and told me to call again in a week's time.

This was in February, and the troops had passed into Zululand some six weeks before. A brief summary of the troops may be of interest to younger readers.

They consisted of four columns.

Col. Pearson, situated at Ekowe, had eight companies of the Buffs under Col. Parnell; six companies of the 99th under Col. Welman; one company of Royal Engineers, with two 7-pounder guns, under Lieut. Lloyd; 200 blue jackets and marines under Captain Campbell, from H.M.S. *Active* and *Tenedos*, with three Gatling guns; 200 of Captain

Barrow's Mounted Infantry; 200 of the Durban Mounted Rifles, Captain Shepstone; Alexandra Mounted Rifles, Captain Arbuthnot; Victoria Mounted Rifles, Captain Sauer; Stanger Mounted Rifles, Captain Addison; Natal Hussars, Captain Norton. A Native Contingent of 2000 under Major Graves.

Two Companies of the 99th posted at Stanger and Durban. This was the Coast Column. Another column was stationed in a strong position, called Krantz Kop, which was almost unassailable. It consisted of a native contingent of 3300, commanded by 200 English officers, with two rocket tribes, under Lieutenant Russell, R.N., and 200 mounted natives.

General Lord Chelmsford's column, stationed at Helpmakaar, was the strongest. It consisted of seven companies: 1-24th, and eight of the 2-24th; six 7-pounder guns; a squadron of mounted infantry under Captain

Browne ; 150 of the Natal Mounted Police ; the Natal Mounted Carbineers under Captain Shepstone ; the Buffalo Border Guard, Captain Robson ; the Newcastle Mounted Rifles, Captain Bradstreet ; 2000 Native Contingent, Commandant Lonsdale ; and 2000 natives under Col. Glyn.

The fourth column, under the command of Col. Sir Evelyn Wood, V.C., consisted of the 13th and 90th regiments ; Weatherley's Light Horse ; Baker's Horse ; Buller's Horse ; Raafs' Corps ; Kaffrarian Mounted Rifles ; some artillery, and a number of natives ; in all, about 2500.

Up to the present there had been occasional severe fighting, especially with Chelmsford's column. After crossing the Tugela River, he fought an *impi*, defeated them, and captured some 500 head of cattle. This was on the 12th of January at Sarayo's Kraal. On or about the 20th, they were encamped at Isandula. The next morning

Commandant Lonsdale and Major Dartnell were ordered to reconnoitre with a force of volunteers, Police and Native Contingent. The day following they sent in word that the enemy was near in great force.

Hearing this, General Chelmsford left early the next morning with the 2nd battalion, 24th regiment, the Mounted Infantry, and four guns, sending an order to Lieut.-Col. Durnford, commanding No. 2 Column, to move on to Isandhlwana camp with all mounted men and a rocket battery, to take over command, as he was leaving with Col. Glyn to attack the Zulu force, reported to be some fourteen miles off. Col. Pulliene was to be in command until the arrival of Lieut.-Col. Durnford.

Durnford received the order too late, and was obliged to fall back, and sent praying for reinforcements, as the enemy had surrounded him in large numbers. However, he managed to get to Col. Pulliene with the news that an enormous force of Zulus was advancing on to their small body.

Indeed, it was but too true. They were the flower of Cetewayo's army, and numbered about 20,000; they surrounded the British camp, and advanced in silence until quite close to it. Then they came on with a rush, yelling their terrible war-cry. There was no resisting them. The mighty, surging mass of naked demons hurled themselves with terrific impetus into the camp, and falling on the soldiers with their stabbing assagais, drove them hither and thither like sheep, stabbing and spearing all before them. Very few escaped from this awful slaughter, the result of a terrible blunder of General Chelmsford's in the first place, and of the officers left in command in the second.

The encampment was on the bare ground, without the slightest attempt at a defence in case of attack. If a *laager*, as at Kambula, had been made, they would certainly have

ZULUS.

kept the enemy at bay until the General came to their assistance, but, instead of that, the force was scattered.

One company of the unfortunate 24th was sent out to meet the Zulus, I suppose for the purpose of trying to check them, and not one returned. The infantry had no chance of escape ; they were simply wiped out. Some of the mounted men escaped across the river ; others were cut off and shot. Col. Durnford and Col. Pulliene were both killed. In all, there were about 800 white men and 200 of the Native Contingent slaughtered ; there were no wounded, as it is the custom of the Zulus to kill their own wounded as well as their enemies.

A part of the victorious enemy rushed on to Rorke's Drift to seize the booty there, and their intention was that the whole army should advance into the Colony of Natal and lay it waste.

In the meantime, whilst this awful defeat

F

was taking place, General Chelmsford and Col. Glyn were engaged fighting a paltry force of 500 Zulus, of whom thirty were killed. Then the dreadful news reached them that the Zulus were in possession of Isandhlwana, busy sacking the camp.

When the General received these disastrous tidings, he sent Col. Glyn forward with most of the troops to retake the camp, but they received no opposition ; and when night came on the weary and dispirited troops lay down to rest amongst the dead bodies of their friends and comrades in the *débris* of the camp.

The next morning General Chelmsford hurried on with his small force to Rorke's Drift. This place was in charge of Lieut. Chard, R.E. In the afternoon two men rode furiously up, and gave the appalling news of the full extent of the Isandhlwana disaster, and stated that the Zulu army was advancing to take the Colony, and that Rorke's Drift must be held at all cost.

Rorke's Drift is on the Tugela River, just below the junction of the Blood River, and is wide and deep; the troops crossed by the aid of large ponts.

Lieut. Bromhead was in command of a company of the 24th there.

Everything now was made ready for the attack. The *laager* was formed of bags of mealies and biscuit-boxes and a couple of wagons. The force, numbering 104, were determined to succeed or die.

About 4.30 P.M. the Zulus were seen advancing, and a withering fire was poured into them; but, elated as they were from their recent victory, they charged undauntedly on up to the very barriers, and wrestled with the bayonets. It was a desperate struggle, but they were beaten off only to charge and re-charge, sometimes almost succeeding in taking the little camp. The fighting continued until 4 o'clock the next morning, then the Zulus, numbering 3000, disappeared over the hills, and the Colony was saved—thanks to the brave defence and pluck of this little company in face of overwhelming odds.

Soon after Lord Chelmsford arrived at Rorke's Drift, and congratulated the gallant defenders warmly.

On the same day that Isandhlwana was fought, Col. Pearson's column marching to Ekowe was attacked at Inyezani along the entire right flank and in front. One hundred and thirty wagons, with a long train of oxen attached, makes necessarily a long column, all the more difficult to defend. However, the Naval Brigade and the Buffs poured out a steady fire and held the position, while the rear wagons closed in. The main body of the Zulus was located in the bush, which was immediately shelled; this drove the enemy into the open plain, where they were effectually routed, and forced to fly to some heights; these were in turn stormed, and a complete victory gained. The British loss was twelve

ZULU WOMEN.

killed and sixteen wounded, while 300 Zulus were slain.

After this nothing of importance occurred until March.

I must now return to the story of my own career. I spent the intervening week in watching the fortifications of the town being made, or rambling through the military Compounds. I often met Major H——, with whom I sometimes messed, and he informed me that we would in all likelihood be sent to the Cape Colony for more horses. I told him that sooner than do that I would join some volunteer corp, which was certainly against my inclination, for I wanted to go to the front and see active service. At last the day arrived. I called at the War Office, where I was informed that I was appointed to take charge of a convoy of wagons on their way to Kambula, and that other duties would be assigned to me on my arrival there. My salary was to remain at 16s. 6d. a day, and

I was to start at once. Hurrying to my hotel, I strapped some things in a valise, and hastened to the Remount Stables to procure a horse. I knew the officer in charge, and he informed me he had not one fit to give me, there being only six in the stables, all on the sick list. I told him I must have one, as I had to catch up a convoy before it reached the Zululand border, so we went to the stables and inspected them. They were indeed a sorry-looking lot, but I chose, as I thought, the best, strapped my valise on a saddle, and started on my long ride.

I was forced to walk my horse most of the way, and until I reached Colenso on the Tugela River, my journey was most uneventful. This place is about 80 miles from Pietermaritzburg, and it took me three days to reach it. Here I learnt a lesson which I have not yet forgotten, but before relating it I must make a few remarks as to what led to it.

During the Zulu Campaign the Commissariat Department was worked in a very different way to what it is now. It is now included in what is called the Army Service Corp; but at that time officers belonging to different regiments managed the Department under Commissary-General Strickland. Amongst the duties of these officers was the purchase of cattle for meat and transport wagon work, as well as large quantities of grain. I heard at different times from reliable resources that the British Government was swindled over and over again by the vendors of cattle and grain, who were mostly Colonial adventurers; the officers buying miserable beasts at large prices, likewise paying exorbitantly for the grain.

After the war I was told by several men, who considered it in the light of a good joke, that a man would take, say, fifty head of *trek* oxen, sell them at £15 apiece,

and get his cheque. These cattle would
be driven into the yard or kraal, stolen by
the vendor in the night, and driven to some
quiet out-of-the-way place. Giving them
there a rest of a few weeks' time, he would
return and re-sell them sometimes to the
same officer. A Colonial or a native would
easily recognise any cattle again ; but one
could hardly expect an officer in the British
army, unused to dealing with live stock, to
do so. I heard of many other swindles in
the same line.

I was very young, and felt enthusiastic
about the war, and everything touching it
roused my keenest interest.

Arriving at Colenso, leading my jaded
horse, which was completely done up ; chafed
at the delay and tired from the continued
walking, I was not in a very cheerful state
of mind. Putting my horse in the stable
of the little inn, I sat down for a smoke on
the *stoep*. Soon after two officers in un-

dress uniform rode up from the direction
of Zululand. The younger man led the
two horses round to the stables, whilst the
elder eyed me from head to foot, answer-
ing a careless nod from me. Presently
he came out, sat down near me, and we
entered into conversation. He told me
that he had come from the front, that everything was quiet there, but the war would
probably be a lengthened and expensive one.
I, with the cock-sureness of youth, launched
into my views of the management of the
Commissariat. It was a most unfortunate
and ludicrous conversation for me, as I had
no idea I was talking to my own General,
and the Chief of the Department in question !
He listened for a while until I had nearly
finished, but at last, when he could stand it
no longer, he jumped up and asked : "And
who the devil are you?" Much surprised, I
told him my name and rank, and asked to
whom I had the pleasure of speaking. He

answered that I had better be careful in the future to find that out beforehand, and re-entered the inn.

I sat and wondered for a while who the man could be, and then went to the stable to see how my horse was getting on. There I met his companion rider, and asked him who the "old buffer" inside was. He answered it was General Strickland! I felt somewhat alarmed, and related the conversation we had, and what I was, at which he laughed heartily, and advised me to get out of the way as quickly as possible. I took the hint, and saddling my horse pushed on again.

Never in my life had I seen such a night. It was pitch dark, and I had to lead the horse and strike matches every now and then to find the road to the river. When I got there another difficulty arose; the pont was on the other side, and I had to shout repeatedly to rouse the ferryman. At last he

came out of his cottage and said it was too
dark and too late to ferry me over. I shouted
out that I *must* cross, and at once, and, as he
still argued, I told him I was despatch-riding
to the front, and, taking out my revolver, fired
off a shot. This and the falsehood had the
desired effect; it bluffed him completely, and
he ferried me over. I put on a good deal of
"side," and abused him soundly for detaining
me with important despatches, forgetting all
the while the appearance of the animal I was
leading. He remarked ironically that it would
be a considerable time before the despatches
reached their destination if I rode that
animal, which made me feel rather foolish.

I mounted and rode on, and could only just
get a glimpse of the wide white road. The
air was hot and heavily charged with
electricity; there was not a breath of wind,
and I expected a thunderstorm. The next
stopping - place was Ladysmith, where I
expected to catch up the convoy, and my sole

regret was that I had not a good horse to push on more quickly. Presently there was a flash of lightning quite close to me, and before the roll of the thunder had passed away repeated flashes were darting about me. Ten minutes later I was in the thick of a good old Cape thunderstorm; flash followed flash in quick succession; the glare of the forked lightning illuminated the night, striking the trees and earth in every direction. My horse, knocked up as he already was, was shivering from fright, and I could hardly persuade him to advance a pace. Near the road I noticed a hut, with a bush-kraal full of sheep. I rode up, dismounted, and asked permission to stay there until the storm had abated. It was a small hut, with seven Natal Zulus squatting round the embers of a fire on the floor. They refused point blank, observing that there was a house belonging to a white man a little further on. I told them they were *Amakafula* (Kaffirs), a term of

A KAFFIR CHIEF.

insult to a Zulu, and rode on. I had no difficulty in finding the house a mile ahead. Meanwhile the rain had come down in torrents, and I was wet through in a very short time. In answer to my loud knock the door was opened by an Englishman, who did not, however, seem inclined to let me in, only that the storm was too bad to turn away a dog. I was surprised at this reception in such a hospitable country, but he apologised for it later on, explaining that he was besieged both day and night by camp-followers and others on their way to and from the front. He had no stable, so the unfortunate horse was tethered to a post outside. We sat up talking late into the night, and it turned out that he had a brother in the old Colony who was a great friend of mine. Upon hearing this he made me very comfortable.

The next morning I was up at daylight, only to find that my horse had taken fright during the night and broken away. It was a very

G

lovely morning, and, as the ground was wet, the *spoor* was easily traced. I tracked him for two miles, and found him amongst some low hills where the grazing was good. On my return my host exclaimed : " It was very lucky for you that you did not sleep in that hut last night, for it was struck by lightning and every man killed." It certainly was a narrow escape, and haunted me for days. I had never in my life experienced danger before, and it had not occurred to me that I was running a chance of being shot or assagaied by the Zulus. The idea would keep coming back, till at length I asked myself seriously if it proceeded from cowardice. I was loath to believe this, and finally reasoned myself into the conclusion that it merely arose from inexperience, and that most other fellows had probably felt it.

After an early breakfast I proceeded on my way, and arrived at Ladysmith in an hour's time, where I saw the convoy camped outside the town.

On reporting myself to the officer in command he handed the convoy into my charge.

I found they had suffered not a little through the storm, having camped on low ground and literally slept in water. Four oxen had been killed by lightning, and they had taken no measures to replace them. Borrowing a horse, I rode round the outlying farms and bought four others, giving the vendors orders to draw the money on the Department. It took me the whole day to purchase and drive the oxen to the camp.

Upon arriving there the officer in command of the troops was angry, and told me I ought to have gone on without them. This was absurd, and so I told him, and gave him to understand that he had nothing whatever to do with the wagons and oxen, they were in my charge, and his duty was merely to escort them.

From Ladysmith we travelled in a north-easterly direction to Dundee; it being my intention to take the new road from there up the Blood River, and save about forty miles.

At Dundee we found that the road was impassable, owing to the heavy rains, and I decided to make for Utrecht, where I knew good roads existed. This led to a fresh dispute with the officer, as he insisted upon travelling the shorter road. I explained to him that, as we had eighty wagons, the leading ones would cut up the road to such a degree as to make it exceedingly difficult for the following ones to get over it, and we would probably take twice as long in reaching Kambula, besides being utterly unable to draw the wagons close together in case of an attack. He flew into a violent rage, and threatened to place me under arrest and manage the wagons himself. I told him we could settle the matter on arrival in camp.

After that we went for some miles on very bad roads, where the wagons sank up to their axles, and it was a case of unloading, drawing the wagons on a little, and loading

up again, only to find the wagons sink
slowly again in the mud after a few yards,
forcing us to unload and reload all over again.
Fatigue parties were told off to assist, and it
took us a week to go three miles. I was
kept busy galloping up and down the line
directing the movements of wagons, or putting on extra teams to force them through.
Sometimes the mud was ploughed up in front
of the wagons by the efforts of thirty-two
oxen, whilst yokeskeys, neck-straps, reins,
were breaking in every direction. To make
matters worse, it poured with rain, but the
men worked through it like demons, digging,
shouting, and urging on the tired oxen. At
last we got on to good roads again, and
travelled slowly until we arrived at Utrecht
to allow the oxen to recover a bit.

We were joined here by twenty more
wagons and some troops sent from Kambula
to meet us. We then marched the thirty-six
remaining miles to our destination without
any event worth recording.

CHAPTER VI.

On the 27th of March a force made up of some of the Frontier Light Horse, Raafs' Corp, Weatherley Rangers, Baker's Horse, the Native Contingent, and other Volunteer Corps, under Col. Wood, started from Kambula to attack Zhlobane Mountain.

Col. Buller led the attack, and, when near the top, the Zulus opened a heavy fire. Several men and officers fell before the enemy were driven off. The rocky mountain swarmed with Zulus firing from krantzes and caves. It was estimated that there were about 10,000 of them, while our horse only numbered 600 besides the Native Contingent.

After a few hours' desultory firing from the summit a large body of Zulus appeared on the north side. Col. Buller rode off to attack them, but noticed presently swarms of natives climbing round the side of the mountain underneath him to cut off the retreat of our men from their only available means of descent. There was no doubt that the main part of the Zulu army had arrived, and he gave the order to retreat.   It was an awkward place to descend, even at a slow pace; but the knowledge that they were surrounded by an overwhelming force impelled the men to dash down the steep rocky incline at full speed. An attempt to rally proved a failure, and the retreat rapidly became a panic. A Zulu lurked behind every boulder, and sprang out upon the white men, stabbing right and left.

Col. Weatherley, a gallant Colonial officer, his son a boy of fourteen, and sixty-six men were cut off, and every man, with the exception of six, was killed.   The former was last seen standing over the body of his dead boy, fighting bravely, a sword in one hand, a revolver in the other, until he fell pierced with assegais.

Our loss amounted to 120 men, and many acts of bravery were recorded, especially on the part of Col. Buller and Captain Cecil D'Arcy.

On the 29th we saw an enormous army of Zulus marching towards our camp. They moved in a dense mass, with a point or horn stretching out on either side. Bugle calls were sounded through the camp; orders were given to finish our meal in haste, and, as the enemy came nearer, the alarm sounded; tents were struck; and every man took up his position on and under the wagons which surrounded the camp. There was no noise or bustle, rather an ominous quiet. Boxes of ammunition were opened and put down next the men; horses saddled in case of need; and a look of grim determination seemed to

grow on the faces of the men, for the sight of
the advancing Zulus called up memories of
slain comrades at Isandhlwana and Zhlobane.

The great dark mass moving steadily on
had now arrived quite close to us, and we
could distinctly discern their dark forms,
when suddenly another column of the enemy
appeared over a rise on the opposite side of
the camp. A mounted force was sent out to
meet them in skirmishing order, amid hearty
cheers. Advancing some distance, they dismounted, fired, and retired; this they repeated. It was done to draw the enemy on,
and get them within range of the guns. The
manœuvre succeeded, and shell after shell
ploughed through their ranks. It was splendid to see how they pressed on without any
regard to the galling fire of the artillery.
Every time a well-directed shell exploded
amongst the densest part, and those around
fell dead or wounded, a cheer would ring out
from the soldiers.

The other column now came up, and we were surrounded. However, we kept up an incessant fire, mowing them down like corn. On they came, making charge after charge, no doubt believing they would gain as easy a victory as before ; but at length they were forced to retire under our withering fire. Nevertheless they struggled to get at us the whole afternoon, but finally gave up and fled the way they had come. They were not let go in peace ; the artillery continued to pour shot and shell into their disorganised force ; the cavalry pursued them for miles until dusk, shooting and cutting them down.

The Zulu strength that day was over 20,000, and nearly 2000 were slain, whilst of our side, numbering about 2500, only thirty were killed and fifty wounded.

The Zulus seemed to fire too high, for their bullets whistled thickly over our heads ; and I should not be surprised, when they were quite close in, if some of them hit some of their own men on the opposite side. They were the same force that attacked Isandhlwana, and had many Martini rifles, taken at the sack of the camp.*

It was after this fight that a few of our men met death in rather an odd way.

Firewood being scarce, we proceeded to collect all the old muzzle-loading rifles and assagais of the dead Zulus. (This, by the way, was rather a ghastly task, as the Zulus seemed to stiffen in their death-struggles into the most extraordinary attitudes.) The stocks of these were chopped up for fuel by the soldiers, and the barrels were found to make excellent grates in the camp fireplaces. Oddly enough, it did not seem to occur to the

---

* It was here that I witnessed a man flogged, and believe it was the last time that this form of punishment was administered in the British army. The man was tied to a triangle, bared to the waist, and thrashed with a "cat" until he had received the number of lashes he was sentenced to. This was done in the face of the whole camp, who were drawn up in order to witness it.

men that some of these barrels might be
loaded, and, consequently, on a fire being lit
under them, many exploded, killing and
wounding several men.

Shortly afterwards the Prince Imperial
was killed. He, six men of Bettington's
Horse, with Lieut. Carey, set out on a
reconnoitring expedition. Having rested at
a kraal to have some refreshment, they were
about to mount their horses when a volley
was fired at them out of some tambookie
grass close by. Two troopers were killed;
the others succeeded in mounting and getting
away, with the exception of the Prince, who
had a tall restless horse, which broke away
from him. The Prince commenced to run, but
was surrounded and assagaied. One pierced
his eye, another pierced him in the side.
In this instance they followed their common
custom of ripping open the stomach. This
is always done by the Zulus and other Kaffir
tribes when they have time; they have been

known to cut out the heart of an exception-
ally brave man, and eat it, from a belief that
it gives them courage.

Individually, I could never see that Carey
was to blame. He did not show any bravery,
it is true, but one man's life is as good as
another's, and this was clearly a case of *sauve-
qui-peut;* he would certainly have been
killed had he remained, and he could not
have rendered the Prince the slightest assistance, as the natives were only twenty yards
away when they fired. At the same time, it
was a dangerous place to dismount, and showed
a lack of military prudence. My opinion was
the common one of soldiers at the time.
Carey was, however, court-martialled, condemned, and sent to England under arrest,
where he was released by the Queen at the
request of the Empress Eugenie.

We had moved our camp some distance
closer to a tributary of the White Umvolosi,
and were consequently only a few miles from

General Newdigate's column which was quartered on the Buffalo River.

His force consisted of 17th Lancers, 21st regiment, 58th, a battery of 5th brigade Royal Artillery, a battery of 6th brigade Royal Artillery, Bengaugh's Native Battalion, Natal Pioneers, and Natal Carabineers.

Here we burnt the great Maquilizine Military Kraal, and captured 9000 head of cattle.

A month later we struck camp again.

During this time I had plenty of work to do in getting wagons into marching order, and in keeping those belonging to different regiments together.

General Sir Garnet Wolseley was now appointed to take charge of affairs in Zululand, both civil and military.

General Newdigate joined our column, and we moved towards Ulundi, where Lord Chelmsford's column was stationed.

At daylight, on the 4th of July, the

CETEWÁYO.

British army crossed the Umvolosi River and camped on the high ground. Shortly after the halt had been made the enemy was seen approaching from two directions. Our troops were formed up in a hollow parallelogram, the Native Contingent in the centre with the ammunition wagons. The four sides were formed by eight companies of the 13th, five companies of the 80th, the 90th, the 58th, and 34th regiments, the 17th Lancers and Mounted Irregulars. At the corners and centres artillery were placed, Gatlings, 7-pounders and 9-pounders.

At 8 A.M., as the enemy was advancing, Buller's Horse met them: Cochrane's Mounted Basutos were sent to 'the right. In one hour the British opened fire, and the brave Zulus pressed silently on through the deadly hail of bullets. Once more they showed their utter contempt for death, and I feel sure there is no nation on earth that would advance steadily under such a terrible fire as did they on that occasion. On they charged, until at a distance of no more than seventy yards, when they could face it no longer; a few rushed on, only to be shot down. The rest hesitated, wavered, and fled. Now was the time. The Lancers dashed out and bore down upon them like a whirl-wind; the bursting shells, the roar of the guns, the loud crackle of the Gatlings and "ping" of bullets, made a most exciting scene. It was the last stand of the Zulu army, and about 1000 were killed. The battle over, the great Kraal was given to the flames. In it was the king's palace, which consisted of a thatched building of four rooms.

After this the Zulu warriors retired to their homes, and the king fled to the moun-tains. A force was told off for his capture, under the command of Major Barrow, who tracked him for many miles. Great activity was shown by Major Gifford, who nearly captured him; at length he was run to

ground by Major Marter, and escorted to
Ulundi. From there he was taken to Port
Durnford, put on board the s.s. *Natal*, taken
to Cape Town, where he was imprisoned in
the Castle.

Peace was proclaimed, settlements made,
and the camp broke up.

I left in charge of a large convoy of
surplus stores for Natal, where they were
sold. There I received my pay, and left
with a good sum of money for the Old
Colony.

CHAPTER VII.

REACHING East London, I went by train to King William's Town, bought a horse, saddle, and bridle, and was once more a wanderer.

At Adelaide, where I stayed a few days, I met a gentleman who had lately arrived from England and started ostrich farming fourteen miles from the town. He was in want of a sub-manager, which post he offered to me. I accepted it, promising to be with him in a week's time. My salary was to be £5 a month ; this, though small, was better than nothing. Mounting my horse the next day I rode seventy miles to Cradock to see Mabel. When the week expired I rode back, to enter upon my new duties with Mr Parker.

I did not like the place from the first; it was wretchedly small, and the birds were few, and not by any means good. He was a good sort : knew very little about farming, and would not take anybody's advice on any subject. He had four incubators, and we incubated all the eggs. This I protested against, explaining that weak chicks would be the result of forcing the birds to lay. He paid no heed to my advice, but maintained that if the birds be highly fed, no weak chicks could be born. I said no more, and simply let things take their course. As I had anticipated, most of the chicks were born decrepit and died; the adult birds suddenly stopped laying, and six months ensued before they started again. In trying to get a large number of chicks in the year, we only got a few, although we had hatched out more than anyone else around. It was a case of killing the goose with the golden eggs. After this, he came to the conclusion that I knew more—at least about ostriches—than he did, and let me have my own way.

He had begun to take a keen interest in racing, and was busy seeing to the erection of large stables for his horses. He spent most of his time now at race meetings, and ill luck seemed to attend all his ventures. One thing was clear to me—as the farm was not paying well, and he was dropping large sums over horses, things could not go on for long as they were. A severe drought followed, and we were obliged to buy grain at high rates to keep the birds alive. At length one day he came to me and said he would be obliged to sell out, as his resources were exhausted. Two months afterwards the sale was held, and I left once more for Cradock. There I met a Mr Gill, who offered me a post on his farm to manage his incubators. I was to be paid at the rate of twelve one-month-old chicks per season, including board and lodging. Twelve chicks a month old at that time were worth £100, so I reckoned that in a few years I would be able to start a farm of my own with the birds that lived, and in the meantime it would be easy to get someone to take them on the half-profit system. This system helped a great many poor farmers, both Dutch and English.

In due time I went to Mr Gill, prepared the incubating-room, boiler, etc., and a month later was busy collecting the eggs from the nests, dating them, and putting them into the incubators. The season was just drawing to a close, and we did not think many more eggs would be obtained, when the Basuto War broke out.

I had worked hard and done well, and Mr Gill was highly pleased on seeing a fresh "clutch" turned out every ten days, and there seemed every prospect of its being the best chick season for him on record.

The new war caused considerable excitement, and orders came that burghers were to be called out, and proceed to the front. Men were picked between the age of sixteen and fifty, starting by names commencing with the first letter in the alphabet. I knew I would not be called out, as I was not in the district when the names were taken.

The men were allowed 4s. 6d. a day, with rations and ammunition. Each man had to find his own horse, or, failing to do so, was supplied with one, and the value duly docked out of his pay. He could evade going by finding a suitable substitute; many did, but it cost them from £20 to £100.

One morning, as I had just finished turning the eggs in the incubator, and was standing idly at the door looking down the valley, I saw someone come galloping along the road leading to the house. Every now and then the rider would disappear among the trees at a bend of the road, to reappear, leaving a cloud of dust behind. I waited awhile, and then saw that it was a lady. On coming nearer, I recognised Ethel Brown, a pretty little governess in a family some miles off, who was engaged to my best chum and oldest friend, one of the finest fellows in the Colony.

I hurried forward to meet her. She jumped off her horse without waiting for my assistance, and exclaimed :

"I can't come in—I only wanted to see you. Walk back part of the way with me, and I will tell you why. I'm so glad I found you at home."

I took the horse and led him. After a few minutes she said :

"Of course you've heard about the Basuto War?"

"Yes," I replied.

"Well, George has been called out," and breaking suddenly down she added, "what shall I do? Oh, what on earth shall I do?"

"If he does not want to go he can find a substitute."

"Yes; but I'm afraid he *will* want to go; and, besides, a substitute costs such a dreadful lot."

"What does he say about it?"

"He is away, and does not even know he is called out, and he has to be ready in a week."

"Oh, that's nothing," I remarked, unthinkingly. "A fellow could get ready in twenty-four hours."

"What an unfeeling brute you are! What about me? Am I only to see him just a few hours before he starts, and perhaps never see him again? You forget we were to be married in a month's time."

Here she broke down completely. I felt an awful brute, and said the first thing that occurred to me.

"I beg your pardon, Ethel; I never thought of that. If it comes to that, he need not go at all, you know, or trouble to find a substitute either."

She looked up with a start of hopeful surprise, explaining: "Oh, what do you mean?"

"Just what I say."

"But he must, Egie; he cannot get out of it."

"Oh yes, he can. Suppose I go instead?"

She exclaimed incredulously, "You don't really mean it!"

"Indeed I do," I said. "I've just about finished with the incubators, and I can easily come to some arrangement with Mr Gill, and so get away for a few months."

Ethel threw her arms round my neck and kissed me, crying: "You darling old boy! you dear! how good of you! I can't say how grateful I am to you."

"Oh, I shall enjoy it immensely," I said. 'I've been sticking so closely to my work here that a few months' shooting, even at Basutos, will be a relief."

"Poor old boy! I don't half like your going. I'm afraid I've been very selfish." She grew suddenly graver. "I have not even told you some news I heard about Mabel; but you must not be upset about it, it is sure to come right in time."

"What have you heard?" I inquired anxiously. "No trouble, I hope."

"Well, you see, her people never liked her engagement to you; they have always wanted her to marry Col. Sinclair, and it seems they promised him to further this as much as possible. Now that your engagement has become public, and he has to go to the Basuto War, they want her to declare her engagement off with you, and marry him in a fortnight before he starts. That is the latest I have heard about it. Poor Mab is very fond of you, and is very much cut up; but what can she do?"

"She might refuse to marry him."

"Oh, yes; but she would never disobey

them. She is like most Colonial girls: she will marry whoever she is told to, and I don't think tears will help much in this case."

I was too distressed to talk any more. I wanted to be alone and think, so I got rid of Ethel as soon as I could. I took my rifle, went along the river, and sat down under a mimosa tree. There was only one thought uppermost in my brain. He was going to the front—so was I. He might be killed in action. The strangest reasonings dashed through my head. All sorts of voices prompted me; I just sat and listened to them as if they were inside me, reasoning and weighing chances, and telling the results to me, a passive listener.

Supposing that during a fierce engagement I were to see him close to me? Supposing I were to find myself alone with him? Supposing he was in range of my revolver? . . .

The kook-a-vic was piping his shrill note in a bush hard by. "Kook—a—vic," kook—a—vic, kook—a—vic." It seemed to me it called, "Shoot—him—quick, shoot—him—quick, shoot—him—quick." I felt half frightened at my own fancies, at the involuntary impulses that awoke in me, and walked hurriedly home. I passed quite close to a steinbok and a duyker, and only realised it afterwards. I never once thought of firing at them.

CHAPTER VIII.

In the market square of Cradock some 400 burghers were assembled. All the inhabitants of the town and the country people for twenty miles around were there for the purpose of saying "Good-bye" to their fathers, or sons, or lovers, or friends, as the case may be.

In a low phaeton, in front of the court-house, sat Mabel and her mother. Colonel Sinclair leant over the side and chatted with them. It seemed to me she was paler than usual, and her eyes were searching anxiously through the crowd of men. It was not easy to distinguish anyone amongst them, as they were all dressed alike—

corduroy uniforms, wide-brimmed felt hats
with red pugarees, a cartridge belt slung
round them, and carbine in hand. They
were mostly gathered in small groups : a few
galloped about the town saying "good-bye"
to such friends as could not leave their
desks or houses to see them off. It was
a glad day to some and a sad one to others.
Twelve o'clock was the time appointed for
the muster. At a quarter to twelve I
walked quickly down the square, leading
my horse, determined at all events to say
good-bye to Mabel. I shook hands with
her, and holding out my hand to her mother
said : "Good-bye, perhaps for the last time,"
but she merely bowed. With an expressive
look at Mabel, and a slight nod to Sinclair,
I turned away. Sinclair seemed rather
amused; he had a slight smile on his face.
I cursed him as I went, feeling as miserable
as any fellow could feel. Being so well
known, every one came and shook hands

with me, and wished "God speed!" and, feeling as I did, I was thankful to see the hands on the court - house clock point to twelve. As the hour was striking the men formed a long line, and a fine lot of fellows they looked—all Africanders, all good shots, sitting well on their saddles, resting the butts of their carbines on their thighs. The captain, accompanied by the sergeant-major, walked down the front of the line and read the roll. Every man answered, and, as the town band struck up, the men waved their hats, passed in sections round the square and down the road towards Basutoland.

What a long miserable journey that was to me! I often felt inclined to put spurs to my horse and gallop off anywhere.

We walked our horses along the hot dusty roads for 450 miles; we could not have gone more quickly had we desired, as our baggage-wagons only travelled at the rate of fifteen miles a day.

I

I was in a kind of daze—one thought uppermost. If I could not marry her myself, I was determined to do my best to prevent Sinclair from doing so. I felt more of a man, more aged, and took things more seriously. For a youngster of not nineteen, I had been through a good deal; had seen and experienced more than falls to the lot of most lads; I was old for my years.

Meanwhile we had camped outside Aliwal North, a town on the Orange River, the border of the Cape Colony and the Free State.

There were few incidents on the march worth recording; the routine was monotonously the same, day by day. The morning march started at seven o'clock until twelve, a halt, and on again at three until seven.

At length we arrived at Wepener, presenting a very different appearance to the smart body that set out. Our neat uniforms were mud and travel stained, our hats and pugarees awry, our hands and faces tanned to a dark brown.

There we heard the news of the breaking out of the Boer War. This caused much discussion amongst the Dutch and English burghers of whom our force was composed, not always of an amicable nature. In the evening, when the men returned from the town, having drunk a good portion of " Cape smoke," a fight ensued, the outcome of an argument as to the merits of the English and Dutch between two of those nations, and ended in a general scrimmage, which lasted over an hour. Of course the English proved best with their fists, and the Dutch were driven out of the camp howling. The officers were powerless to do anything; indeed, as they were for the most part Dutchmen themselves, they preferred not to interfere in the row. The Dutchmen as a rule are not plucky.

At Wepener we waited for reinforcements. They flocked in almost daily from Somerset, Graaf Rienett, Middleburg, Bedford and Colesburg; and when about a thousand had joined, we struck tents and marched on. A few miles brought us over the boundary into Basutoland proper. The wagons were drawn four abreast, no matter how rough the ground over which they had to travel. The men, each with 200 rounds of ammunition, rode on either side. An advance guard of six men rode half a mile in front, the officer in charge being allowed a certain amount of discretion. The train was also followed by a similar and rear guard; scouts rode parallel with the column on either side. We had proceeded a little more than half way to our destination when the advance guard was attacked under a sugar-loaf-shaped hill, called Kalbani Kop. We heard their firing; the alarm was given, and the men stood with loaded carbines in front of their horses, laggard oxen were thrashed up by frightened native drivers, and in the space of a few minutes the wagons formed in a compact mass. The advance guard soon came galloping in, and two or three hundred of the enemy made their appearance. Upon these we promptly fired, without making any visible effect. Coming to the conclusion that there was not a stronger force of them in the background we moved on, slowly and carefully, but they harassed us for many miles, taking advantage of every scrap of cover to send bullets amongst us. One man was shot through the head and four wounded; several unfortunate oxen were dropped, which caused delay ; we had no time either to take the meat on with us, which would have been useful, but contented ourselves by dragging them out of the way of the rear wagons. We had yet twenty-one miles to go before reaching our destination, and ten miles a day was good travelling under such circumstances.

I remember that it was very hot, and that there was a good Cape thunderstorm in the afternoon. It poured cats and dogs, and we slept that night round the wagons on the wet ground in our wet clothes, with belts and pouches full of cartridges, with our carbines by our sides, fully expecting an attack. However, the Basutos were kind enough to give us time to rest, and we were up and stirring at first glimpse of daylight. The day that followed was a lovely one, the roads were good, and the enemy not very troublesome. Now and then a stray shot would be heard from the advance or rear-guard, and we could always see some of them hovering round out of range.

At about seven o'clock that evening we arrived at Mafeteng, where I found, to my surprise, that Col. Sinclair was in charge of the garrison, which consisted of all the Cape Yeomanry and some native levies under Captain Bowker. We went on about two

miles further, and camped on a low flat hill
with a fine lagoon at the foot of it.   Then
with the usual bustle the wagons were
formed into a square ; an outer square
surrounding this again was made by building a sod wall, four feet high, with a space of
twenty yards between it and the wagons,
our tents being pitched in this space.   For
the next week, and indeed during most of the
campaign, it poured with rain.   There was
mud everywhere, and our clothes were always
wet.   .

The whole country round was dotted with
ant-heaps, averaging a circumference of ten
feet.   These were always perfectly dry, as
the outer surface is smooth, hard, and water-
proof.   The inside resembles a huge honey-
comb ; thousands of tiny passages intersect it
in every direction ; these passages are almost
filled with minute pieces of dried grass.   We
made holes in the top in which we placed
our pots and kettles, then broke a hole in the

crust at the foot, and lit a fire there. The whole ant-heap would soon become like a furnace, cooking our meals excellently. A good-sized ant-heap would serve as an excellent stove for a whole week. After these gave out we were in sore straits for fuel, the enemy doing their best to prevent us from getting any, and generally succeeding. We burnt grass roots and dried the droppings from the cattle; the latter made good fuel, and competition for it was keen.

A day or two after our arrival I rode over to the Mafeteng camp, and met a few fellows I knew. We had a great deal to tell each other. They had evidently had a rough time of it. When they formed camp they mustered a small force — three hundred with the artillery. The Port Elizabeth infantry were under Col. Carrington, and were near Dephiring; the rest at Maseru. The Mafeteng camp was surrounded at once. It was almost certain death to fetch water from the

spring close to it. Relief was so slow in coming that they had run short of provisions and
were eating their horses, and Boer brandy
was more plentiful than water.

If a horse happened to stray it was soon
seized by the Basutos, who dashed out on
their smart little ponies and seized it. These
natives are, I may add, always mounted.
They are the horse-dealing tribe of South
Africa.

Two officers of the Yeomanry played a
trick on the enemy. One night they went a
short way out of the camp with a horse, and
having hobbled him, hid in some bushes.
Just after daylight the horse was noticed by
the Basutos; three of them dashed down,
dismounted, and were taking the hobbles off
when they were shot by the officers, who
hastily mounted two of the Basuto ponies
and galloped back to camp, amidst the cheers
of a crowd who witnessed it. Such were some
of the stories with which I was entertained.

A few nights afterwards I was asleep in my tent when I was roused by several shots being fired by the sentries. I was half dressed, and seizing my sword and revolver rushed out. The men were rushing from their tents, and crowding to the outer wall, firing off their carbines at random in the darkness. At least the Dutch were. We did our best to check them, but as they were not used to discipline, and the greatest cowards imaginable, it was of little avail. The guard was questioned. He said he had seen several black forms creeping towards him, that he had stuck to his post and fired several shots at the enemy. There was no doubt of it: the man was in a state of abject fear without any real cause for alarm. I walked back disgusted to my tent, the Dutchmen having fired several hundred rounds out of sheer fright. The enemy must have been rather amused at our expense, for they have, I fancy, some sense of humour.

One miserable dark wet night they tied a lantern to the neck of an old lame horse and let him loose, about half a mile from the camp. The swaying about of the light gave the Dutch an idea that the enemy were advancing for a night attack ; accordingly, they kept up an incessant fire. But the old horse fed stolidly on, unheeding the bullets flying around him. The captain, Mynheer Van Wyk, was much excited, and showed great bravery on that occasion—actually had the daring to exhibit himself over the wall. When daylight came the old horse was seen quietly feeding, little realising the excitement and acts of bravery of which he had been the innocent cause. Some of the Dutchmen actually wrote home to their wives, telling them how they fought the enemy in the dead of the night and beat them off, and nothing could persuade them to the contrary. No doubt it was very amusing to the fellows in the other camp as well as to the enemy, but I was getting heartily sick of the whole thing. These night alarms occurred several times ; but at last one day the men had an opportunity of fighting in earnest. Orders came from Col. Carrington that 300 burghers were to be at his camp at daylight the next morning for a reconnoitring and wood-collecting expedition. The captain was on the sick list, so I was told off to take charge. I may state I now held a lieutenant's rank, and was about the only one who had seen any active service. Starting at half-past two A.M., we arrived in good time, and were immediately joined by a company of the Cape Mounted Rifles, some artillery with four 9-pounders, also an ambulance wagon, and three transport wagons, the latter for the loading of firewood. About an hour after we had set out (we were riding in sections along a ridge), some 2000 Basutos appeared on the top of another ridge close by : they had evidently no intention of leaving us unmolested. We halted, and waited till the whole body came well in sight. Our 9-pounders, concealed by a body of Cape Mounted Rifles, were got ready for action, under Captain Giles. Orders were then given to us to retire in the opposite direction, the guns remaining. The ruse acted admirably, as the enemy thought we considered their force too strong for us. We had scarcely begun to disappear when the remainder of the force followed us. The Basutos poured down the hill in a black mass. Our guns were halted, and at a distance of about 500 yards opened fire with good effect. The enemy retreating, we galloped back and pursued them. We could hear the shells whizz through the air over our heads like giant bumble-bees, and see them burst on the opposite hill. There was a general scatter of the Basutos whenever a shell exploded amongst them, and they would rush in another direction, only to be met by a fresh shell. This demoralised them, and by dint of hard galloping we managed to cut off about fifty of them. At a distance of sixty yards we sprang off our horses and sent a volley amongst them that unhorsed several ; then suddenly, to my surprise, they wheeled quickly round and charged us, waving their assagais in the air, and yelling out something I could not catch. The reason for this change was soon apparent; just behind us the entire body of the Basutos was bearing down on our small force. I saw that there was only one course open : to charge and meet the smaller force, cut through them, and get back to the wagons. I wished in my soul that I had Englishmen under me instead of Dutchmen, as I knew they were not to be relied upon in a case of this kind. Plucking up heart, I shouted out the order ; but it was of no use, the men simply turned and fled to the left, down the valley. There was nothing left for me to do but go also,

cursing them soundly. I almost felt as
if I could willingly have joined the Basutos
and helped them to fight.

There was now a body of the enemy on
either side of us, coming ahead like the wind;
their active ponies, used to the rough country
and unhampered by harness or heavy riders,
were cutting us off with ease. Suddenly I
saw another body of horse coming towards
us. My heart sank, and I felt that all was up
if they turned out to be more of the enemy.
I was determined to blow my brains out
rather than be taken prisoner. Stories were
common of the treatment received: how one
man had all the tendons in his legs and arms
cut and torn out; another was stuck with
assagais by the children until he died a
lingering death, and so on. A moment later
I thanked God that this new body of horse
was the Cape Mounted Rifles coming to our
assistance. It became simply a mighty race
for life; four troops of horsemen racing as

hard as ever they could go. A collision was inevitable, so, gripping our revolvers, we crashed into the thick of them. It was a tangle of men and horses. As far as I could see, the Dutchmen seemed neither to attack nor defend themselves, but simply dug their spurs in their horses' sides and endeavoured to get away. I emptied my revolver, then slashed about with my sword ; assagais were flying thickly. Two lads, sons of a farmer I knew well, were both killed just in front of me. An assagai struck me on my side, but only made a flesh wound, as my sword belt saved me. One fellow rushed at me with his assagai raised, but I succeeded in cutting right through his hand and the shaft with a cut from the left shoulder.

We would, undoubtedly, have lost heavily but for the timely arrival of the Cape Mounted Rifles, who finally routed them. We lost six men and had eight wounded.

After that we found it utterly impossible

to get any wood from the sides of the hills, as the Basutos were all round us, and harassed us on every quarter. Fresh bodies, too, were arriving every moment to strengthen their force. We then returned to camp, and, as a matter of course, I was blamed because the men bolted.

A fortnight after that we had a similar outing, without, however, coming to such close quarters.

On this occasion the Dutchmen distinguished themselves by their shooting, and bowled over a good many at remarkably long ranges.

Affairs were getting desperate. After another interval we sallied forth again—this time with a much stronger force—to attack a stronghold. These strongholds were made on the sides of the most rocky hills, and were rendered almost impregnable by the erection of a series of short stone walls, or "sconces," overlooking every point of vantage

K

behind which the enemy were sheltered. The Basutos were armed with the best rifles, and owned any amount of ponies and cattle. They are the most wealthy of all the native races in South Africa.

We went out eight hundred strong to take one of these places. I saw, with not a little satisfaction, that Sinclair was to join with some of his Yeomanry. After marching a few miles, the enemy came out to meet us as usual, and welcomed us with a few shots, which we answered with our 9-pounders. This little exchange of amenities was kept up for the next five miles, until we arrived, at eleven o'clock, close to the place we purposed attacking. The spot seemed quite deserted, but we knew well that behind those little stone walls amongst the rocks thousands of black fellows were safely ensconced with loaded rifles, besides fragments of rock ready to hurl down on our heads.

We had no sooner reached the outer wall

when the whole place swarmed with black figures, and a terrible fire opened on to us. However, over we went, scrambling over the rocky walls, stopping every now and then to fire a shot. Shells were flying overhead from the guns and mortars : the explosion of these, combined with our determined rush, had the effect of making the enemy bolt. We had actually taken this wonderful stronghold that was so much talked about! It was however, of no use to us just then, so we destroyed a good deal of it, leaving about 200 of the Basutos dead. As the enemy were in great force that day, we expected some more fun. Shortly after this we saw about 100 natives on a low hill watching our movements. It was right in our line of march, and, on coming near them, the order was given to charge. We were in the centre, the Cape Mounted Rifles on our right wing, and the Yeomanry on our left. We had ridden a little more than half-way up, when suddenly about 8000 Basutos poured over the top of the hill. Of course my men turned and bolted like rats, but the native ponies cut them off in a minute, notwithstanding the shelling. The wings closed in, and then we had our toughest bit of fighting. It was a hand-to-hand struggle for fifteen minutes. How I escaped being killed was a wonder. During all my feeling of intense excitement, the thought of Sinclair kept coming to me, and I was searching for him all the while—I did not know clearly why.

Meanwhile I received a blow from a battle-axe that nearly struck off my knee-cap, but did not inconvenience me until afterwards.

Someone dashed against me from behind and nearly unhorsed me. I felt intuitively that it was Col. Sinclair. I had one cartridge left in my revolver, and I raised the latter. I could not help it; I was not master of my actions; something impelled me to fire—urged

upon me that it was my duty. I pressed
the trigger—the whole thing did not take a
second. As I pressed it, a Basuto close
behind hurled an assagai at me ; it struck me
just below my forage cap, and was fast im-
bedded in my skull. Following up his throw,
he rushed at me with a *knob-kerrie*, and dealt
me a thundering blow on my head, which felled
me to the ground. The fighting continued
for a few minutes longer ; I was semi-
unconscious. I felt one of the enemy seize
hold of me, strip me of my sword-belt, and
take the revolver, of which I still had a grip.
I was lying on my face, the blood pouring
from the wounds in my head, so that my face
was in a puddle of it, yet I was unable to
move ; indeed, had I done so, it would have
been certain death, as the enemy kept
passing, almost trampling me with their
horses' hoofs.

Finally the natives were beaten off. It was
getting late and misty, and a slight drizzling

rain was falling. Everything was quiet
except for the boom of the guns firing every
now and then at the retreating mass, and the
occasional groan of wounded men. "Good
God!" I thought, "they are moving away."
Such was indeed the case, and our side was
retiring towards the camp. I struggled to my
feet, and tried to wipe the congealing blood
out of my eyes; everything was dancing
before them, but at last I could see our men
disappearing over the hill. I endeavoured to
run, but found walking even beyond my
strength. I fell to the ground with a thud
that opened my wounds afresh. My knee,
too, was stiff and painful. After resting a
few moments, sucking the wet grass, which
revived me a little, I crawled along on my
hands and knees in great agony. Going
through some rather long grass I heard the
thud of horses' hoofs, and crouched down
in it. Presently some Basutos dashed past,
not a hundred yards from where I lay. They

were following our men who were in retreat.
The sound of heavy firing told me of the
renewal of the fighting.   Crawling ahead as
fast as I could, I saw a fierce struggle going
on   below.   Once   more   the   enemy   were
beaten off ; I could see them retire in the
opposite direction.   Our side waited in a
square, anticipating another attack, and in
order to pick up the dead and wounded.
This gave me a chance.   I struggled on as
fast as my lacerated knee would allow me,
until I was forced to give in, and could
not get a yard further.   Half kneeling, half
fainting, I waved a handkerchief.   Luckily for
me, it was seen.   Three officers of the Cape
Mounted Rifles — Capt. Cecil D'Arcy was
one—came out and helped me in.

There was no room in the ambulance
wagon, it was crowded with wounded ; even
the open wood wagons were laden with dead
and wounded.   I was laid on to one of these,
shaking like a leaf.   An infantry man took

off his coat and put it over me, remarking consolingly that I looked like "pegging out"! If his words carried no comfort his coat did!

Yet once more the Basutos charged, and lying in the wagon I watched the progress of the fight, not caring a "doit" what happened. They were driven off again. It was getting dark, and we had seven miles to go over a rough country. There was a dead Kaffir driver lying next to me, smelling so horribly that my faintness increased. Dr M'Lean then came up. He was one of the finest fellows I ever had the pleasure of meeting; he was badly wounded on the head and body himself, but he had bandaged himself, and had attended to the wounded through the thickest of the fight. He showed great pluck and endurance that day, and deservedly got the Victoria Cross for it. He examined my wounds, and having dressed them, remarked that the wagon I was in was

no place for a badly wounded man. On going
to the ambulance wagon he found a fellow
had just died, and he put me in his place, then
made a start for the camp. The jolting was
most excruciating, and it was pitiable to
hear the groans and curses of the wounded.
We pushed right on to Mafeteng, where the
hospital was, into which we were put.

I lay on my face for nearly a week, while
the surgeon probed for splinters of bone. Capt.
Bowker, of the Native Levies, took rather
a fancy to me, and I owed many comforts to
his kindness during my stay here. On the
journey in the ambulance wagon I recognised a friend, named Blaine, of the Cape
Mounted Rifles. He, poor fellow, was
assagaied through the body, and died in the
bed next mine the day following. The whole
thing seemed like a dream to me; I was
dazed, and unable to realise the course of
events.

We lost over twenty men that day, and

many were wounded. My escape was considered miraculous, and I was not a little amused at the newspaper accounts of it.

Colonel Carrington received a wound from a spent bullet while returning to camp, but it was slight.

I made inquiries about Col. Sinclair, and heard he was sound and well. Was it some special providence that had caused me to be wounded just at that moment, and saved me from——well, murder? I like to think it was.

I lay for weeks in the hospital in a very uncomfortable bed, cursing my luck, for peace had been proclaimed. Col. Sinclair and his Yeomanry had returned to the Colony ; most of the burghers had deserted, and the rest disbanded. As soon as I was able to hobble about I bought another horse and fed him up well, preparatory to my long ride.

I reached Cradock in four days, my horse knocking up at the end of the journey.

I found the town deserted; everyone had gone to the race meeting, which was at that time one of the best held in the Colony. The race-course being only three miles away, I borrowed a horse and rode out to it. In the ring in front of the grand stand I was greeted by everyone (for they had all heard of my escape) with congratulations. As I did not see Mabel in the stand, my first question naturally concerned her. I was told they had married a few days before, and were away on their honeymoon. What I felt is better imagined than described, so I will not bore the reader with any more of my love troubles. Suffice it to say, I felt as all youngsters do, that life was no longer worth living.*

---

* I met a man afterwards who had served with me in this war, who informed me that he had received fifty shillings in prize-money from the Colonial Government. I had not applied for any, not being aware of any large captures of cattle, and had merely been compensated for

Before ending this chapter, it may be well to say something as to the cause of this war. It arose out of the enforcement of the Native Disarmament Act, an absurd Act passed after the Kreli War, 1877-79, for the purpose of depriving the natives of their firearms. The ridiculous part of it was that the natives did far more damage with their assagais than their guns, most of them not being able to shoot at all. One officer, who had been through the Kreli War, told me how he had met suddenly one of the enemy in the bush. The native, who was about twenty yards away from him, raised his piece, fired, and

---

the loss of my horse. As I was only slightly higher in rank than this man, and did not think there would be much difference in our awards, I offered to sell him my chance for £3, to save myself the trouble of applying. He accepted the offer, applied, and obtained £11 ! It turned out that there was " blood money " due to me, a Colonial custom of which I was ignorant.

missed. My informant then promptly shot him, and, on examining the Kaffir's rifle, found that he had the sight fixed at 700 yards. The Basutos refused to comply with the Act, and hence the war.

CHAPTER IX.

HAVING received an invitation to stay with some friends in Grahamstown, which, by the way, is my birthplace, I accepted it. Giving my horse a few days' rest, I rode down and spent a quiet month. Whilst there I was unfortunate enough to lose my horse through the terrible Cape horse-sickness. It is known by no other name than "horse-sickness," and has hitherto defied all veterinary skill to find a cure for it. It generally attacks a horse in the summer, and they rarely survive it. As to the symptoms, the belly tucks up, the eyes become large and glassy, the animal froths at the mouth and nose, and dies apparently in great agony in the course of a few hours. It is strange how they sometimes turn instinctively to man when this disease attacks them. My friend had an unbroken horse which was particularly wild, and would let no one approach him. One day we were leaning on the gate of the field where this horse was running, when suddenly we saw him walk slowly towards us. He came right up and laid his head against my shoulder, breathing heavily; his nose and mouth were covered with sticky froth, and he was trembling all over. We kept quiet, and I felt his head get gradually heavier and heavier, until I could scarcely support it, then at last he suddenly fell, made a slight struggle, and died. To us, who were passionately fond of horses, it was a sad sight.

Another curious sickness which attacks cattle is the *dronk siekta*. It is caused by eating a kind of grass called *dronk* grass. Eating it induces a comatose state, from which the animals do not recover unless quickly attended to. The only effectual antidote known is some form of alcohol. A transport rider told me that he had once emptied three cases of gin into a " span " of his oxen which were thus affected, with good results.

Seeing no prospects of getting employment, I resolved to try my luck at the gold-fields, which were then attracting considerable attention, and reports of good finds were in constant circulation.

L

A BOER TREKKING.

CHAPTER X.

THE coaster left Port Elizabeth at four o'clock P.M, and arrived at Durban at the same hour on the third day. Staying there a day or two at the Royal Hotel, I went on to Pietermaritzburg, and then by mail cart to Newcastle. I left my luggage to come on by ox wagon, and never saw it again.

Then, to save money, I arranged with a transport rider to pay five pounds for a lift in his wagon as far as Leydenburg, a distance of 240 miles. On the second day we crossed the Umzinyati on Buffalo River, which takes the name of Tugela, on reaching the border of Zululand. *Trekking* up the steep hill, we saw where the Boers fired on the ambulance

wagons as they descended with wounded
men, on their way to the hospital at Newcastle. Reaching the top, we saw Langs
Nek and Majuba Mountain, the scene of the
disaster which put an end to the Boer War.
Near here we passed a stone monument,
where thirty-three officers and men fell in a
few minutes under the unerring aim of the
Boers. Crossing the Ingogo River we outspanned, and I strolled up to a store near the
bank to buy some provisions. I found the
proprietor an intelligent man, who had
remained unmolested in his shop through
the entire war, and witnessed not a little of
the fighting from his door.

I had a long conversation with him, and
found his ideas agreed with mine in refer-
ence to this war. The proper way to fight the
Boers is either in their own way, or by attacking them at night ; keeping persistently
after them by forced marches if necessary.
The English soldier is a bad shot under the

easiest of circumstances, and when marched into the open to face bullets that are directed with unerring aim, and drop his comrades one after the other, giving him no chance to retaliate, as no enemy is visible, only here a hat or there a puff of smoke behind a rock, what chance has he? He can but run away (which he *did* do), or stand and be killed.

On the other hand, in night attacks Tommy Atkins is as good a shot as any Boer. Only one thing would be needed : a gallant charge with bayonets. The Boers, who are arrant cowards, would certainly retreat on horseback, leaving their wagons, oxen, spare horses, ammunition, and provisions behind them.

In a great many instances their wives and children were with them in their big tent wagons.

The Boers could not retake the camp, and would not even try ; as long as their ammunition held out they would shoot at long ranges

in the daytime, but they would never risk a
fight at close quarters or in the dark, having
only their unequalled shooting to rely upon.
What a chance General Colley missed! If,
instead of climbing up Majuba with no
sensible object in view, he had marched along
Langs Nek to the enemy's camp about the
same distance away, I really think the war
would have been ended there and then in our
favour. I heard afterwards that the Boers
knew the English were marching that night,
and, fearing an attack, had inspanned their
oxen ready for retreat, but this they would
have found impossible. A hundred heavy
wagons would have great difficulty in getting
away across such rough country in the dark.

But, instead of that, what happened? When
daylight appeared, the Dutch, to their great
surprise, discovered the English on the top
of Majuba, waiting, as it were, to be shot at.
In a very short time the Boers surrounded
them, and creeping up behind the stones

picked off their men with the greatest ease, and the least danger to themselves.

After this defeat the Government disgraced the British army by suing for peace, which was declared, and then the army slunk quietly away, leaving the Boers to insult and sneer at every Englishman they came across.

Travelling on, we steered for the town of Leydenburg, where we arrived after having been twelve days on the road. We saw a good deal of game on the way—springbok, blesbok, and a few hartebeests.

Leydenburg is a pretty little town, consisting of two long streets running parallel with each other. It was the scene of some fighting in the Boer War, the English camp being almost within rifle-range of the town, which was *laagered* by the Boers. Firing was constantly kept up without much damage resulting to either side.

One painful and curious incident occurred at this time. As is well known, if a sentry on active service is found asleep at his post, he is liable to be court-martialled and sentenced to be shot, especially at a time and place where danger is imminent. One night a sentry in the —th Regiment was discovered asleep at his post, which was situated between the two camps. He was court-martialled, and condemned to be shot at sunrise. The day broke ; he was escorted to a spot in the camp, and all the troops were mustered to see the sentence carried out. There was breathless suspense, and, just as the command to fire was about to be given, a stray bullet from the rifle of a Boer whistled through the group of officers and men, and shot the prisoner through the heart !

Every house in this town has its large garden well stocked with peach-trees, bearing a rather hard though juicy yellow fruit. Leydenburg is situated right in the heart of the gold formation, and "colour" can even be found in the dust swept from the streets.

I was surprised to find there a friend of
mine, who had just arrived for the purpose of
trying his luck at alluvial digging. We
agreed to go to the De Kaap Valley and
work together, and, like all beginners, were
eager to commence, imagining that it was
more profitable and easier worked than
it is. There were a good many diggers in
town, with some of whom we soon became
friendly, and we listened eagerly to their
wonderful stories of mining — how they
found gold every day with the greatest ease
—all the usual lies told to greenhorns. We
agreed to take one with us as a mate, to
share in our fortunes and teach us the science
of gold-digging. We started one day on our
forty miles' walk, crossing over the " Devil's
Knuckles," a hill shaped like a clenched fist,
and on the second day passed through the
" Devil's Kantoor," a village under canvas,
where we bought our tools, some boards, provisions, and took out our licenses. Hiring a

bullock cart, we started down the mountain-
side to the valley below, where we could see
many tents dotted about.   Reaching the foot,
we pitched the tent, and I took back the cart.

Our first work was to go prospecting,
which is the most difficult part of gold-
digging. Our new mate certainly under-
stood his work, but I did not care for his
company, and I resolved to dissolve partner-
ship at the first opportunity.   Every day for
a fortnight we would try fresh places—sometimes in shallow gravel, sometimes in the
terrace of a creek, or a dry gully—carefully
lift the " wash " of the bed rock, carry it to
the nearest water, and pan it off.   We nearly
always got " colour," but not in paying
quantities.   At last, one evening, we struck
good " colour " in a little creek, and returned
home to pack up, after pegging out our claims.
Our home did not take long to get ready
with the help of a pile of wood which we cut
on the side of the mountain.   We worked

like slaves, eager to start at our El Dorado.
Our next proceeding was to make a "tail
race," that is, a fall from our claims to carry
away the earth and fine gravel, otherwise
"tailings." This took us three days' hard
work, standing up to our knees in water,
working with pick and shovel. That finished,
we made a "head race," about 200 yards
long, from the claims up the side of the
creek to a favourable place for the building
of a dam. That was another three days'
work. The next day saw the dam finished,
and then we started to wash off the earth
from the gravel, which process is called
"stripping." When this is done, a sluice-
box is fixed at the lower end of the claim in
the "tail race." This box is generally
twelve feet long and twelve inches wide, and
paved with rough stones, leaving plenty of
crevices between which the gold can settle.
One man then stands at the head of the box
with a twelve-pronged sluice fork with which

he loosens *débris* in front of the box, and causes it to wash away, and forks up stones of a certain size, and throws them over his head on one side of the claim. The larger stones are thrown up by hand, the boulders smashed with a sledge-hammer. This work goes on until the "paddock" is washed down to the bed rock, generally a week's work, then the clearing up commences. The bottom is generally a blue micaceous substance, that cuts like cheese, upon which the gold lies. The top of this is carefully skimmed off with a spade, and placed in a heap near the head of the sluice-box. A few stones are taken out to enable the fork to be worked easily. Less water is now used than before, and the wash is slowly forked in the box. This finished, the stones are lifted out of the box and washed, in case any gold is sticking to them. The contents of the box is then scraped into pans, which, when "panned off," leaves the object and result of the week's work exposed.

Our first "wash-up" amounted to nearly an ounce of gold, worth about £3, 5s. It was disappointing, but we hoped for better luck next time. Another week's work gave us 10 dwt., worth 35s. Talking the matter over·that night, we decided to do one more week's work, and then, if no better result issued, to prospect for another place. The next wash-up brought less gold than before, and the claims were given up.

We had become short of provisions, and our new fellow-workman proposed to go into the Devil's Kantoor, sell the gold, and buy the necessary wants. He went the next day, and Dick and I did a little fruitless prospecting. Arriving home that night, we found our mate had not returned, and came to the conclusion that he had drunk too much "squareface" (Hollands), the general drink there. The next day there was still no sign of him, so we went supper·less to bed, there being no food left.

·Hungry. and annoyed, we set· out the next day. to look for him, but found no trace. Making inquiries, we heard he had disposed of .the gold for five pounds immediately on his arrival, and was afterwards seen on the road leading to Leydenburg. He was, we also heard, one of the biggest scoundrels in the gold-fields, and went by the name of ."Long Tom." It was no use in following him for so small an amount, but we rather prized it as the first result of our digging experiences. We saw a good many diggers about camp; a number of these were "fossickers,"—that is, men who pot about creeks and places scraping the dirt from under boulders and out of crevices with their pan, and washing it in the nearest water, making a few shillings daily.

We dined in a canvas eating-house, where there were about twenty other diggers eating, drinking, and swearing. It contained a long table with forms on either side, a large pot at one end of the room slung over the fire. As a man came in a tin plate was taken by the proprietor, who was cook as well; this he piled up with a mixed kind of stew out of this pot by the aid of a huge fork and ladle, clapped it down in front of the customer with a tin pannikin, and demanded half-a-crown. If he wished for tea, it was sixpence extra. Such tea it was too, stewed to a black liquid, and no milk, except condensed, to be had! Some of the men brought a pint of gin in their pocket, and emptied it into a pannikin. The heat was fearful, and the place swarmed with flies; but we were hungry, and, finishing our "dollop," as they called it, as quickly as we could, were glad to get out of the reeking place into the fresh air.

After buying provisions at the stores, the storekeeper, to whom we had confided our affairs, said he knew of a claim for sale which had been paying well, and the owner

wished to go back to his home. We walked
about a mile to where the claim was, and
had a talk with the owner. It was the last
claim at the head of a worked-out creek.
Trying the wash, we found fair prospects
in the pan. He asked £50, and we
eventually bought it for £35 and a suit
of clothes. The bottom under the worked-
out claims was all soft "blue," and I noticed
that in the last paddock he had finished
it was a hard yellow rock, and seemed to
shelve up, making the wash shallower as
it went on. This was a puzzle to my in-
experienced eye, and I was rather afraid;
but not knowing what to do or where to go,
we thought we might as well risk it.

Paying over the money, it left us with
only £5 between us, and it was necessary
to hire a native to help us at £1 a week
and his food.

The next day we moved our camp over and
commenced work. At the end of the week

we washed up, and, to our intense disgust, found only five dwt., worth 30s. We paid the boy, bought more provisions, and, as the monthly license had expired, had to take out fresh ones, which left us penniless.

Another week's wash-up resulted in no gold whatever beyond a few "colours." We went to the storekeeper with our tale of woe, and he advised us to try another week at it, and gave us credit for provisions at large prices, and paid our boy.

It was Sunday, and leaving Dick asleep I strolled down to the claim to have a quiet smoke, and think. Looking at the hard, cracked bottom a desire seized me to break through this and see if there was any difference in it a few feet under- neath. Seizing a pick, I managed to heave up a large three-cornered chunk of flat rock, and, to my surprise, I saw yellow gravel underneath. Rushing back to the tent I quickly roused Dick, and told him of

M

my discovery on our way to the claim.
Regardless of it being Sunday, we dug a
lot of this out, and panned it off, and soon
a shining rim of gold, more than we had
ever found in a week, lay round the edge
of the pan.

It was barely daylight the next morning
when we set to work, and in three weeks
we had taken out over £800 worth of fine
gold. We were only sorry it did not last
longer, but it was encouraging, and we
never worked harder in our lives, not
breathing a word about our luck to anyone,
for fear of the claim being "jumped," which
was no uncommon thing in those days, there
being no law whatever other than Lynch
law, and disputes often settled by fights.

Digging is exciting work; it amounts
to a craze, a fever. There is always
the chance of a big nugget or a rich
"pocket," such as the one we found. In the
summer it is almost certain death to go down

into the low country, yet I have seen men who could not resist it, but go to their fate to some reputed rich ground. Four went down from the Devil's Kantoor while I was there. A fortnight later one of them returned a wreck, physically ruined; the others, he said, were dead.

The claim exhausted, we were again stranded with no work to do; we half contemplated going to a "rush" a few miles off, but waited for better news of it. On a visit to Leydenburg to bank our money, I met a man who had a large concession in Swaziland, and he offered me the post of agent there. I was to receive a small salary, have food supplied, be allowed to work the creek for my own benefit, and receive payment of £1000 on the event of my discovery of a payable reef. Similar terms were offered for Dick. We consented, and started on a seventy-five miles' walk, with two Shangaan natives carrying our

"swag." There was no road, and we walked
in single file along the narrow bridle-track
with the mountain peaks to guide us. Passing out of the Transvaal into Swaziland, I
saw one of the most beautiful sights in
Nature I had ever seen. The border
between the two countries is formed by two
distinct mountain ranges, which are part of
the Great Drackensberg, which extends
1000 miles along the eastern side of South
Africa.

We arrived at Kamhlubana Peak to cross
the border, and here we found a natural
bridge stretching from one range to the
other. This bridge is a vertical rock formation, crossing a valley of about 2000 feet in
depth, is 20 feet wide, and 200 feet in length,
with trees and bushes growing on it. On
either side we could see the deep, narrow
valley winding its way for miles amongst a
rugged confusion of mountains. The sides
were thickly grown with trees and under-

growth of creepers and ferns, amongst which was the *baviaan tau*,* studded with its thick sharp thorns, and strong enough for a ship's cable. Cascades were crashing their foaming way through the rocks, dashing the rain-bowed spray far out into the valley. It is called the Devil's Bridge, and why so many beautiful places are named after His Satanic Majesty I can never understand.

On the fourth day we arrived at our new home, a pretty grass bungalow on the edge of the creek. We found the provision wagon had come, and stood outspanned, ready for unloading. We spent the week in making camp bedsteads and chairs, and getting our Robinson Crusoe home comfortable.

We found a quantity of goods for trading with the Swazis, such as knives, axes, beads, and coloured stuff. The beads were

---

* Baboon rope.

of three kinds, but they would only have one sort, a little ruby one which they called *umlilo-wan* (the fiery one). The cotton stuff was blue, and blue with red stripes; they preferred the latter, and called it *malenkamp;* the other they called *tyodo.* Salt was in great demand; they gave us a quart of milk for half a teaspoonful. It was curious to see them lick it out of the palms of their hands. Salt being so heavy, and the journey so difficult, made it an expensive article. Mealies, honey, and native potatoes they brought in quantities. The latter vegetable is a round dark-brown root, with a thin tough skin; it grows like a small shrub, and is very prolific. After boiling for two hours in two waters the skin becomes loose, and it is fit for table. We found it a delicious vegetable, and I should think, with cultivation, it would improve and become a favourite dish in Great Britain, where it would grow well, as it is suited to

ZULU CHIEF AND WIFE.

the high and cooler parts of Swaziland.
They called them *matapan*. They also
brought us gourds, sweet potatoes, beans,
twyala (beer), *habane* (bananas). The
beans were of two kinds, *tinshlubu* and *tinsh-
lumio*. Money at that time they did not
understand the use of, and would never take
any. One day one of them brought me a
sixpence, and wanted to buy a blanket with
it. He seemed very disappointed when I
laughed and shook my head, and told him it
was of no use. He ran off gesticulating
wildly, and waving his assagais and sticks,
talking angrily to himself. He had evidently
been defrauded by some trader, and had
probably given a couple of goats for it.
There are three kinds of *twyala* (beer) : one
made of *amabele* (Kaffir corn or millet),
umbila (maize), or the two mixed. We preferred the latter, but took some time to acquire
a taste for it. It looks as repulsive as pig-
wash, and they sit round, drinking gallons

of it out of large black earthenware pots,
and smoking and taking snuff.   They are not
great smokers of tobacco, but use another
plant that has a large percentage of opium
in it, the smoke of which they inhale, then,
filling their mouths with water, spit it out
together with the smoke, through a reed.
They become intoxicated from this dirty
habit, and shout out the most utter nonsense
between the whiffs.   They manufacture their
snuff out of home-grown tobacco, the ashes
of burnt aloe leaves, and a plant called
falani.   It is very pungent.   I took a pinch
once—but never again!   I never sneezed so
much in my life, much to their amusement.

A chief is called *inkosi*, the chief man
at a kraal *umnumzana*, an officer under a
chief *induna*.   These three men have the
right to wear the head-ring encircling the
top of the head, which is made with great
care with their own hair (or rather wool)
and bees' wax, then polished with a prepara-

SWAZI WOMAN AND GIRL.

tion made from the leaves of a plant called *lotsana*.

Boys (*umfana*) or men without wives and cattle (*amahobo*) are not entitled to a head-ring.

The married women (*umfazi*) wear a black skin petticoat to the knees, called a *kaka*. The young women (*entombi*) wear beads round their waists, with several strings of them hanging down in front. Girls up to ten years old wear nothing at all.

They are a social, hospitable people, and many a night when far from home, shooting or prospecting, they have given me food and a hut to sleep in, making me as comfortable as possible in their way, asking me numerous queer questions, carefully examining my clothes and watch, uttering exclamations of astonishment and delight like children. Sometimes they played strange music on their chief instrument, called a *gubu*, which is something like a one-string banjo with an empty

gourd for a drum.   A few women would beat
time gently with their hands, sitting in a circle
round the player, who struck the strings
with a wand, and softly chanted a song,
which I noted was generally about their
cows.   A weird sight and a weird song I
thought, as I sat and watched them with the
light of the wood fire flickering on their
faces.

They are a most moral people in every
way, and it is a very rare instance when a
man seduces a girl.   They are generally put
to death, and if the man leaves any property
it is given to the father of the girl, to whom
it is a financial blow, as he has lost all chance
of selling her.   Theft is almost unknown, and
punished by death or exile.   Their religion is
to do what is right, which is what we call
"right" also.   Lies are rarely heard, and
to tell one is considered a disgrace.   They
know there is a God and call Him *Utixo* and
Nkulunkulu, the highest of the highest.

They have a great belief in their king or queen, whom they say is inspired by God, and think he causes rain to come and go, causes good or bad crops, and anything else by his great power—and the king himself really believes it too.

An amusing instance occurred a short time after I arrived. There was a great drought raging—almost an unknown circumstance there. King Umbandine was implored to cause rain to fall, as their crops were failing, and starvation would ensue. He said it could only be accomplished by his people offering him cattle, and *indunas* were sent throughout the land collecting from those who would give, and a large herd was presented to the king. He then caused large quantities of *twyala* to be made, and many beasts to be killed. All the chiefs were then invited to the feast, and they gorged and drank to intoxication, and the drunken king, smeared with red ochre, covered with skins and ostrich feathers, danced and yelled round a large fire, and invoked rain. After this had been kept up for three days and three nights, the king proclaimed to the people that rain would fall in four days. The people were delighted, drank more beer, and sent messengers round with the good news to their wives and daughters, singing the praises of the king throughout the night. The fourth day dawned, and with it came no rain to fall on the thirsty land. There was great wailing among the people, who asked the king whose fault it was. He told them that some of his people had given no cattle, and until these arrived no rain would fall. The *indunas* rushed forth again, searching for those who had not given, and brought back many more. So the feast continued, and the king went through the ceremony again, and declared that rain would fall before seven suns had passed. On the third day rain fell copiously, and the people praised their God and king.

The religion suits them, and my life amongst them always forces me to ask, Why interfere with it? This inquiry brings me to the vexed question of Missionaries. Most men who have lived with the natives, and with whom I have spoken upon this subject, are agreed as to their harmfulness. They tell the native his belief in his king is foolish, nay, wrong. They destroy it, they break up a religion absolutely suited to the nature and character of the people, and replace it by Christianity, which experience has proved has a demoralising influence upon them, when it has any at all. They teach them reading, writing, and arithmetic; and old residents are agreed the more they learn of our so-called civilization, the less they advance in real civilization. Discontent with their lot replaces happy content; vanity replaces simplicity; and European immorality, a simple, good code of morality. Our code of morals, as practised—as preached, it

N

only exists in isolated cases—is far below their standard; they have no system of prostitution.

The system for marrying their women is admirably adapted to their needs, and indeed for the protection of the latter. An *indoda* has as many wives as he can support, and they are all honest women; at home the European *indoda* has one legal wife, and as many as he can pay for in dishonour.

It is impossible to defend our system, or explain it to a native mind.

Logically, we ought to begin at home, and it is a colossal impertinence and a sinful waste of money—with an East End such as ours, the statistics of bastards we return, and the system of prostitution, which is hopeless, facing us at home — to try to foist our religion upon a people who have one of their own in every way better suited to them. Rather take a lesson from them, and make our roads as straight as theirs. We go from sin to purity, and destroy a virtuous people, body and soul, in the name of religion. In olden days white women and children were always safe with the South African native; not so, I am told, nowadays; we have taught them, by violating their women, to disrespect ours.

As with the other native races, the women do most of the work. . Fortunately for them, the richness of the soil enables them to reap good crops by doing little more than scratching the surface of the earth with their hoes. The herding of the cattle is done by the boys. The men have almost exterminated the game by their system of surrounding a piece of grass and setting fire to it, knocking over the animals as they rush from the flames. They are very fond of this, which really has as much sport in it as beating up a field of partridges in England. They crack jokes, laugh, and chaff each other, and all are in good humour. Everything falls a prey to their unerring aim—bok, partridges, and *pauw*. After the grass has been burned, quantities of *pauws* (wild turkeys) assemble to feast on burnt locusts, grasshoppers, lizards, etc. There are two distinct species of them—the bush *pauw*, and the *vlakke* or veldt *pauw*. The average weight of the former is about twenty-five pounds, the latter about fifteen pounds. The plumage of both is similar, and they are beautiful brown birds, and excellent eating.

To these burnt places Dick and I would go and often secure one or two of these welcome additions to our larder. Upon the mountains, we were told, there were many eland and other game, but we had no opportunity of going to shoot them.

Some days Dick and I worked in the Creek with our man, and others we spent prospecting. The gold we found was but little, but it was better than being idle.

One day I stayed at home, determined to be busy at nothing more or less than an attempt to make myself a pair of trousers. I found it more difficult than I imagined, and was just finishing a most extraordinary-looking garment when Dick burst in, with his pan full of quartz. He seemed very excited, and told me he had found a good reef about three miles away, with gold showing in the stone. The next day we went to see the place, and almost every-where we broke the surface quartz there was visible gold.

It was lucky finding a reef so easily, as it is generally very hard and tedious work. Striking the gold, for instance, in a creek, the prospector works up, testing the nature of the gold with his magnifying glass yard by yard, and sees it change from round, worn specks to thin, flaky, ragged ones. He then knows he is nearer the reef. Then, if the gold appears worn again, he knows he has gone too far. Going back, he prospects the sides, sinking shafts, digging trenches, and continually panning off. Sometimes the result is the finding of a "leader," or a reef that is not a payable one to work, and all his labour has been in vain.

We had lived here now two and a half years, and were anxious to leave, so Dick started to walk to the Devil's Kantoor with the servant, to inform the owner of the discovery of the reef, leaving me alone.

Not caring to do any more work, I started out every day with my rifle, calling often at kraals scattered about the country. One day I was sitting in the doorway cleaning my rifle when a white man staggered up as if drunk. I caught hold of him and helped him on to Dick's bed, and could see at once what was the matter with him. He had the fever badly. I dosed him with quinine, and got him to swallow some soup. The poor fellow was shaking with ague, his head throbbed with pain, and he seemed bad with dysentery also. He told me where he had been : down in the low valleys where we had done some prospecting the winter before. He spoke particularly of a certain valley that I knew well. It had always struck me that the formation here was so different, but not being at all well up in geology I did not know what it indicated. This man, with a knowledge of geology, saw a possibility of finding emeralds there, and risked the descent. For three days he worked there, sleeping high on the mountain-side, but the precaution was of no use ; the malaria fiend seized him, and now he seemed doomed to die. His labour had not been in vain, for out of his belt he took and gave me a small but beautiful emerald, advising me if he died to work in the valley in the following winter. Three days afterwards he died, and with the assistance of a Swazi I buried him in a pretty spot under some huge rocks. I have never been to seek for the emeralds yet, putting it off until circumstances prevented me, but it is my intention to do so some day.

It is not a valley to which one could direct another, as it lies amongst a thousand others in a wild, mountain-tossed country.

A few days after this incident Dick returned with the owner to thoroughly test the reef. This took us a fortnight to do, and it was proclaimed payable.

We then gave notice that we were leaving, and in a few weeks were starting on our walk back to Leydenburg.

I told Dick about the emeralds, and we came to the conclusion that we had better learn something about the method of obtaining them before going.

Walking along, we noticed the slow native method of hoeing the land instead of ploughing, and an idea struck me that, if we invested in a plough, oxen, and a small wagon, we might do well in ploughing for the natives.

Dick thought so too, and we discussed the plan thoroughly, and resolved to put it into operation.

Arriving at Leydenburg, we were paid over the thousand pounds for finding the reef, which swelled our banking account.

We next invested in a small twelve-foot wagon, for which we paid £40; six trained oxen, £84; one plough, £6—the latter a high price; £20 more for provisions, and we were ready.

We were obliged to take a different route, as no wagon could cross the mountain or the Devil's Bridge. We found, however, a good wagon road, taking us as far as Lake Chrissie, then by turning due east through New Scotland, we arrived once more at the mountains which surround Swaziland. Here the Komati River runs in between the two ranges. Going in advance, I found the easiest track down the side of the mountain, and led the oxen, after skidding all four wheels. It was a fearful place to descend; one ox broke his leg, the wagon capsized three times, and one of the plough-hurdles snapped off. We shot the ox, skinned it, and went struggling on. It took us the whole day to reach the river, where we camped for the night.

Having crossed the river the next morning, we had many difficulties to overcome in ascending the opposite mountain, with only four oxen inspanned; but we accomplished it by dint of hard thrashing and hard work. Dick was disgusted, and regretted that he had ever returned to Swaziland. I was confident that we would be paid well in cattle for our ploughing.

We were quite exhausted when we reached the top, and glad to rest the night there.

The next morning one of the oxen was missing—whether it was stolen, or, being badly tied up, strayed, we knew not. There was no chance of following its *spoor* as the ground was dry and hard ; we searched the whole day, but without discovering a trace of it. Here was another loss, and Dick more disgusted than ever.

One more day's *trek* brought us to our destination, which was a disused hut that had been bought for prospecting purposes. Our servant slept under the wagon, and we succeeded in making our grass hut quite cosy, by lining it inside with canvas and hanging a curtain before the door. We spent the next three days in calling at different kraals, telling the natives about the plough ; how we could turn over more ground in one day than they could in a fortnight, and arranging to show them how it was done on a specified day.

They were sceptical as to our ability to carry it out, and on the morning appointed they arrived in hundreds to see this wonderful *indaba* (affair), as they called it. We ploughed a piece of land lying close to our hut, and the astonishment of the Swazis was very amusing. They kept at a respectful distance at first, as if in fear, then gradually came closer and closer, until at last they surrounded and followed us, taking up handfuls of the freshly-turned earth, and uttering exclamations such as *Au ! Alala ! Mababu ! Mame ! Yeka !* and so on.

They were both delighted and satisfied, as were we. They held a great palaver on the matter in their huts that night, and some of them came the next day to ask our terms. We told them we would plough for three days for one head of cattle. After a good deal of further discussion amongst themselves one of them agreed to let us plough three days for him. We went next day and started work. When we had finished it we asked for our payment. However then the fellow did not seem at all inclined to pay up, and expressed his doubt as to whether the land we had ploughed would grow any crops at all ; and no one else would give us work—until they were satisfied that *it would do so!*

It being autumn, we suggested that he should sow some grain or any other crop he wished, and we could wait until the shoots came to the surface before claiming our payment.   To this he agreed, after half a day's hard talking, and we saw that the mealies were sown at once.

In ten days' time the shoots were well over the surface, and we claimed our ox, which he very reluctantly paid, for we found that they now doubted whether the crops would be as good as they were from their own mode of cultivation.   We were disgusted and disheartened at their incredulity, and Dick urged me to return with him to the Colony.   I held out, but promised to go with him as soon as we had paid our expenses, which meant about fifteen head of cattle.   It was my intention, if the plan worked any way well, to start another plough, and break in the oxen we earned from the natives as we went along.

We had now run short of meal, and were obliged to kill the young ox that had been paid to us as the price of the ploughing. We then succeeded in obtaining a fresh contract to plough about fifteen acres of unbroken soil. This was rather a risky undertaking, owing to sunken rocks and tough roots, which might damage the plough, and so place us in a fix, as there was no means of getting it repaired.

The first day's work ended satisfactorily, but on the morning of the second the plough caught in a large hard root, bent to one side, and broke the landside in half. This made all further ploughing impossible, and foreseeing further troubles ahead, we decided to leave the country, and try a more pleasant occupation — or return fortified against accidents. We saw the possibility of making the ploughing pay well, as the Swazis were rich in cattle, and attach small value to oxen, as they will not buy wives, and they had never used them for working purposes. It was our own fault; we had been careless and mismanaged the whole affair. We ought to have had more oxen to start with, and more than one plough, and been provided with materials and tools to repair them in case of breakage.

We informed the natives of our intention. They expressed regret at our leaving them, but assured us, at the same time, that they knew our scheme for ploughing would not succeed, as the witch doctor had said so!

Their belief in their "men of magic" is simply marvellous. In some way this is justified, as these fellows are really clever in their own line. They are generally old men, with white hair, surmounted by a curious skin cap. They sling strings of bones, pieces ot

wood, shells, teeth, and birds' claws in a fan-
tastic way about their bodies, and carry a skin
bag filled with various dirty-looking curiosities. A witch doctor seldom speaks, and,
when he does, it is in a dogmatic tone, accom-
panying his remarks with dancing, gesticulating and weird shouts ; this he carries on
until forced to fall to the ground from sheer
exhaustion, frothing at the mouth with excitement. His word is law, and the people hold
him in dread. He is supposed to smell
out criminals. This is generally easy enough,
as the culprit's fear is mostly so apparent
that he can be detected at once. But the
umtakati takes time over it, casts many spells
about the suspected person, and goes through
a lot of "hocus-pocus" before denouncing
him. He always finds a man or woman,
whether guilty or not. He cures or attempts
to cure illnesses, for which he receives a goat
or two in payment, and will drive the devil
out of a person's stomach, in case he has

taken temporary quarters there, for like payment—in fact, he has the monopoly of a paying business, and has only to demand food whenever he requires it.

We started off once more, with no definite idea of what we were going to take up next, reached the border the same evening, and camped at the river. It commenced to rain as night fell, and kept on steadily until noon next day, and we found the river so swollen that we decided to wait until it cleared off. No such luck; it kept on unceasingly for several days, until finally, as the river was not very wide, we made up our minds to take the wagon to pieces and swim the top part over by the aid of logs, letting the oxen pull across the wheels. Inspanning the oxen, and stripping ourselves of our clothes, we drove down to the water's edge. There we unloaded everything, and with the aid of levers detached the upper part of the wagon without difficulty. Then, driving in the oxen, we let them swim the lower part over. This was not very easy, as the current was unusually strong, and we landed a hundred yards lower down upon the opposite side. Recrossing with the oxen, we let them loose to feed, and started collecting dry logs to swim the remaining portions of the wagon over ; there being so much iron prevented them from floating. Lashing the logs together, I swam across with a rope attached to the raft, and tied the other end to a tree. It took us all we knew to launch our craft, but when once we had succeeded it swung over nicely, although it took us all the rest of the day to land it. Then the oxen had to be fetched and tethered. This done, we supped on bread—fearful stuff of our own making—and coffee, and flung our tired bodies down upon the ground among our scattered goods. We had been working all day under a broiling sun, and were so burnt and blistered that it was painful to come in contact with even a soft blanket. I longed for a cool sheet to wrap myself in ; I had not slept in a properly-made bed for years.

The next morning we proceeded to swim over the rest of our things, such as had to be kept dry. This we did by holding up a parcel in one hand. We kept it up all day, and when evening came we had not half finished.

Once as I was swimming over, holding up a coat, Dick yelled out that there was a crocodile behind me ; I dropped the coat and struck out for dear life. Dick seized his rifle and fired just as I landed ; he declared he struck it, and in any case we saw no further signs of the brute. ¯ He stood on the bank ready to fire, whilst I swam to and fro, expecting every moment to be seized by the leg and drawn under. I do not think I ever swam so fast before or since. The next morning we made a raft, as a quicker means of transport. I was feeling wretchedly ill that day ; the burning sun scorching my blistered body, and the want of good food was having its effect upon me. I was obliged to stop every now and then to retch, my hand shook, and I had a splitting headache ; indeed, I often suffered from the latter since I had been wounded. I stuck to the raft until we got it finished, but then had to give in and go and lie down.   Dick was not affected in any way, except that his body was blistered, and we could pull the skin off in strips. I got gradually worse, and by night I was quite delirious, in a raging fever. Dick declared afterwards that I swore most horribly, and talked of emeralds.   It was impossible to work the raft alone, and the Shangaan servant we had was too wretched a swimmer to be of any assistance, so he was sent off with salt and beads to buy some milk for me. Our provisions were all finished, and there was no game about. Dick had serious thoughts of killing one of the oxen to make broth for me, only that doing so would have prevented us

from getting the wagon up the hill again.
He took his rifle and shot a lot of small birds
with bullets, having no shot gun, boiled them
into a sort of soup, and forced it down my
throat for the best part of a week. We drank
this and milk, whenever we could get it,
eagerly.

There were quantities of a large tree
growing about there, which bore a juicy
berry ; these we found very good eating. We
also got a few wild plums and a berry called
musane. These we practically lived on.

On the fifth day I regained consciousness,
but was unable to move. I found Dick had
swam most of the things over, the river being
still swollen, as rain had fallen at intervals.
Dick urged me to try and cross the river with
his assistance, as staying in that fever-stricken
place, without good food of any kind, and no
human beings within ten miles of us, was too
risky. Making a tremendous effort, I reached
the edge of the water by resting my hands

upon his shoulders ; we succeeded in reaching the other side, although I nearly slipped away from him once or twice. Arrived at the bank, he dried me, wrapped me in a blanket, and dosed me with hot bird-broth.

The weather was intensely warm, but I felt chilly and weak, and had it not been for Dick's care I am convinced I would have died. Poor old fellow! he will never read these lines or know how grateful I am still for his goodness! What befell him I will relate further on.

CHAPTER XI.

WHEN all was ready for a fresh start, Dick explored the mountain side and found another *trek*, which, though longer, was far easier than the one we had descended by.

In some places we crossed the incline was so steep that we had to insert poles through the wagon rails, and use them as levers to prevent a capsize.

At Lake Chrissie we found letters awaiting us. One of Dick's was from a brother, asking the former to meet him on his arrival from England; he was coming out with the intention of shooting big game, and was anxious to form a party for the expedition.

Of course Dick and I promptly jumped at this proposal—and why not? We had no work, no home, no ties of any kind. We accordingly sold out at Newcastle with little loss, and getting into the mail-cart arrived in due course at the Royal Hotel, Durban.

There I was introduced to Dick's elder brother. He was much older than either of us, a fine specimen of the best type of English sportsman.. We soon became good friends, and after dinner we sat down in what seemed to us luxuriously easy chairs, in the quadrangle near the fountain. Indian servants brought us coffee and cigars, and Dick and I felt it was not half a bad thing to taste civilization once more.

Meanwhile we discussed the trip. It turned out to be a more expensive matter than we anticipated. After buying a large tent-wagon, eighteen head of oxen, provisions, rifles, ammunition, and counting for various items of expense before we would reach the goal, it would cost us each about £300. However, we were so keen on joining that we did not care to consider the cost. We made up our minds to make all the necessary purchases in Pietermaritzburg, and left the next day for that town.

I still had my Shangaan servant, Imbandu, who, though perhaps not very intelligent, was hardworking, honest, and very attached to me. We engaged three more to act as cook, wagon-driver, and leader.

In ten days' time we were crawling along the white dusty road I knew so well, on our way to Matabeleland. No pleasanter mode of travelling could well be found than to sit on the box of the wagon, pipe in mouth, no cares, jolly companions, good roads, plenty to eat, drink, and talk about—just letting the time slip by. We generally travelled by night, and in the early morning; before the heavens were stained with the flush that heralds the rising of the sun, we had eaten our rusks and drunk our freshly - brewed coffee, and were rolling across the plains.

What quantities of game there were about at that period! thousands and thousands of springbok and blesbok dotted the veldt. There was no fear of running short of meat. Here and there a *pauw* could be seen, and the cracked guttural note of *koorhaan* was often heard.

One day, just before outspanning, we saw a great cloud of dust, and could just make out the forms of springbok in it. They were making straight for us. Several men were galloping on both sides of the crowd ; every now and then one of them would jump off his horse and send a shot into the enormous herd of bok, then mount and gallop on with them again. I never saw such a number of bok together before or since. There must have been close on 20,000 of them. They had evidently been chased for a long distance, and fresh numbers had joined the original

flock as they went on.   We filled our pockets
with cartridges and waited for them.   They
were getting quite close to us now, and I
became seriously alarmed for our safety ; it
seemed impossible that such an enormous
herd could turn aside quickly enough to avoid
running into us.

Telling the others to follow my example, I
fired a couple of shots in front of the leaders,
which had the effect of making them swerve
slightly, but the terrified boks in the rear were
pushing the foremost ones ahead.   We fired
again, and every bullet told.   Then came the
crash !   I shall never forget that sight.   The
leaders, trying to stop or turn aside, were
knocked down and trampled upon ; they
surged up against the wagon — a living
wave of striving beasts—almost lifting it
up.   Hundreds of others dashed across
these, and leaped over the oxen.   Some
got mixed up with them, until there was a
struggling mass of antelope and oxen.

Several of the latter were injured, but, fortunately, not seriously.

Presently the men who were pursuing them came up and stopped to help us with our frightened beasts, which were straining and smashing the yokeskeys right and left. They turned out to be six Dutchmen, who lived near Heidelberg. They said they had chased the bok for ten miles, had shot over a hundred, and had a small wagon coming along to pick them up. I quite believed the first part of their story, as their horses were just dropping with fatigue; the sweat, too, was pouring off them, and their sides were cut to pieces with repeated spurring.

On the veldt folks do not always wait to be invited to a meal. The nine of us were soon sitting round a large dish of various meats fished out of the stock-pot. The stock-pot was an institution we always kept up. A small one was used when travelling, and a giant when in camp. In it was thrown meat of every kind—venison of many kinds, fowl, legs of mutton, beef, and birds of all sorts. In camp it was always kept simmering over the fire, and popped on at every opportunity when travelling. It was very useful, as there was always a meal ready, enough for a large party too, if required.

After leaving Pretoria we went on for a long distance without seeing any game. We had camped by the roadside, opposite the house of a Boer farmer. Noticing that he had a large number of poultry, I strolled up to the house for the purpose of purchasing a few, as the stock-pot was almost empty.

He turned out to be a morose, impertinent old fellow, refused to sell anything, and as good as warned me off. Going back to the wagon, I saw that some of his fowl were feeding close to it, and I determined to get even with him. I opened my portmanteau and got out some fishing-tackle, and handed each of the other fellows, who had witnessed the interview, a line and fish-hook. Dropping the canvas over the side of the wagon facing the house, we decoyed some of the fowl to the other side by a few calls and some scraps of bread. Baiting our hooks, we then fished for them out of the wagon, and very soon landed half a dozen fat hens. This angling went on whilst the boys were busy inspanning the oxen, and we were off long before the—well, to give it its proper name —theft was discovered, if ever it was.

Another incident on the road is worth mentioning, if only to give some idea of the Boers' treatment of their servants. We met a Hottentot one day, who seemed ill, and in great pain. He was in rags, and in a very dirty condition. Giving him a "soupe" of Boer brandy, he told us he had run away from his master on account of the ill treatment he had received. He showed us great weals on his dirty skin, where he had been thrashed with the *sjambok* (raw

hide strip). He further stated that on the
previous day they *krinked* him. This is the
most dreadful punishment that can be in-
flicted. I had heard of the Boers doing it
before. The head of the victim is tied to
the off hind wheel of a wagon, and his feet
to the off front wheel. The pole is then
pulled over to the near side. The torture
entailed by this process is somewhat similar
to that of the old-fashioned rack.

This was by no means an isolated case.
The Boers' general treatment of the natives
is simply barbarous. They rarely pay them
the wages due to them, and if the unfortunate
servant attempts to run away to a better
situation, he is caught, flogged unmercifully,
and not infrequently shot or otherwise mur-
dered, if any active resistance is attempted.
The Transvaal Boer is a low, murderous,
incestuous (I use the word in its most literal
sense), cowardly demi-savage—I speak now
of the "Dopper" or "Trek Boer"; the Free

State Boer is somewhat better, whilst those in the Old Colony, called Dutch-Africanders, are almost on a level with the English Africander.

We were now ascending into the high country about Rustenburg, and wanted to strike the Crocodile River at Marico Drift, cross there, and follow the river until we came to the northern spur of Lobomba Mountains, in Gazaland.

It was well into the month of May, and although the days were intensely hot, the nights were so cold that the water froze in the cask that was slung under the wagon. We had some good sport before reaching the river, with hartebeeste, oribi, and other game.

Crossing the drift one morning, we mounted our horses and rode out into Khama's country. There we were disappointed at not seeing more game, and missed everything we fired at.

The wagon had gone on by road, so we camped that night near the Notwani River. I can remember well what a still cold night it was. The silence was so deadly that it became intensely irritating ; it was only broken now and then by the bark of a prowling jackal, and once or twice by the distant roar of a lion.

The next morning the leader took the oxen out to graze between the road and the river, where the grass grew best. He soon came running back to say that he had seen the *spoor* of a large animal quite fresh, on the river's bank. The two Marstons went down towards it with their rifles, and left me in charge of the wagon.

To the left was a range of hills running parallel with the road, and as I lay on the ground smoking, I saw four rheabok, of the grey species, walking down the side, and making for the river. I saw that they would cross the road about four hundred yards away,

P

if not disturbed. Telling the servants to keep quiet, I reached out for my Martini, and lay quietly on the ground.

They were walking in single file, stopping every now and then for a nibble. I fired at the largest, and dropped him. Later on, I shot a steinbok from the wagon, and several birds for a collection I was making.

The others returned, and reported that the *spoor* was that of a rhinoceros, which they tracked along the river to the spot where it had crossed; but as the crocodiles seemed to swarm there, they had decided to return, so I had better sport after all.

We had not yet reached good hunting grounds, so we pushed on towards Shoshong without any event of interest. Between Shoshong and the Lotsani River, a distance of 25 miles, there are some hills, at the foot of which we camped for the night, hoping to get some sport on them the next day. We heard lions again that night, and the next forenoon three of us, leaving Dick with the wagon to push quietly on, walked over the rugged hills, thickly strewn with huge boulders.

It was about one o'clock, and I was having a rest, munching a bit of "biltong" as I sat, when I noticed the hindquarters of some large animal standing behind a rock in the shade. I concluded at once that it was an eland, and, holding my rifle in my left hand, went on quietly with my lunch, though never taking my eyes off the spot. I must have sat there for an hour, waiting for it to move, so as to get a shot at its shoulder, for it was useless to attempt to shoot at its hindquarters. Getting impatient, I crawled quietly up to the rock, which was only a hundred yards away. There I found myself in no better position than before, as he would run in a direct line from me if I showed myself, and most probably escape. Picking up a stone, I threw it over my head, so as to let it drop just behind him, which it did ; the buck sprang forward, and I fired a snap shot and pierced him through the heart.

The eland is the largest of its tribe, measuring sometimes sixteen hands in height. Its horns are about two feet long, in two spiral turns, and it has a dewlap that hangs to its knees; it is generally of an ashen-grey colour. The cow eland has no dewlap, and is of slighter build than the bull. All hunters are agreed that the flesh is more delicious than that of any four-footed beast in the world. Looking down at the huge beast, I was considering how I should convey some of the meat, when I heard the crack of a wagon whip in the valley below. Walking a short distance, I saw our wagon proceeding leisurely along the road. When it had reached the nearest point I hailed it, and beckoned to the driver to come to me. We skinned the eland, and carried off a hind quarter, the head, and skin. It was too hot to go out again, so I lay on the wagon and dozed until sundown, when the others joined us, staggering under the weight of four grysbok, which we gave to some natives in exchange for some mealies for our horses.

We slept that night near the Lotsani River, and heard lions again quite close to us, so we kept two large fires going in case of attack.

The following day we took two rifles each, and one servant, and started in search of them, keeping parallel with the road.

Having walked for some hours without seeing anything, except a few small antelope, which I did not molest, I came upon the fresh *spoor* of two lions. I called the others, and we proceeded to trace it for nearly a mile, only to lose it on some hard *brak* (brackish) ground.

The wind was blowing rather freshly, and I knelt down to light my pipe in the shelter of a clump of bushes. No sooner had I struck a match than two lions bounded out of the same bushes, and made for the open. Seizing my`rifle, I let fire at one of them, which was rather a foolish thing to do. The bullet struck him in the jaw. The lion stopped, roaring with pain, pawing his cheek with his huge claw. I was about to fire again, when he turned suddenly round and bounded towards me. Holding my rifle to my shoulder until he came close, I waited. Suddenly he stopped, and crouched for a spring at twelve paces, with his head on his paws, his eyes glaring, and his body quivering. I could see the blood dripping from his mouth. The whole incident only occupied a few seconds. I knew that if my shot failed, it would be all up with me. Aiming just between the eyes, and rather low, I fired and he fell over, dead. It was my first lion, and I was astonished at my own coolness as I stood looking at it, with my unlighted pipe in my mouth. It was only a little while

MATABELE WOMEN.

afterwards that I began to feel shaky with excitement, and I could not have hit a haystack if I had tried.

We skinned him, and my man wrapped the skin round his shoulders, leaving his hinds free to carry my heavy elephant rifle.   -

We then went down towards the river, to some low-lying, marshy ground, where I expected to find a rhinoceros.   We walked round the marsh, as the ground was too soft to venture crossing it.   On the north side is a small *krantz* overhanging the river.   Up this we climbed, and we had a fairly good view from the top of it.

At first we could see nothing, with the exception of a great crocodile basking in the sun on the opposite bank.   Presently I heard a shot quite close to me, and hearing a plunge, I ran to the edge and looked over. There, in the river, I saw a noble water-buck swimming down stream.   It was evidently one of the Marstons who had fired; and as the buck was bound to escape at the rate it was going, I seized the advantage of an easy shot, just as it was about to land.

It staggered, fell, and rose again, and started off at a most remarkable speed along the narrow strip of strand between the *krantz* and the river. Another shot—a most lucky one—shattered its skull between the horns. Waiting for Marston, who came running up, we found his shot had struck it in the flank. It had a fair pair of horns, about twenty-five inches with the curve. We took some of the meat with us, but found it afterwards not at all good to eat.

Dick Marston had shot a duyker, which we found a much more palatable substitute.

Between this and Tati we shot a few more antelope of different sorts, and found many *spoor* of rhinoceros on the banks of the Macloutsi River.

Leaving Tati a week later, we entered

Matabeleland, and passed through some beautiful country. Marston shot a sable antelope one day, which had a splendid pair of horns. We lingered in the neighbourhood for some days, hoping to get another out of the half-dozen he had seen, but they disappeared in a northerly direction.

We came across a small herd of gemsbok one afternoon, in a small valley. This was somewhat strange, as they are generally to be met with in the open country. We stationed ourselves one on each side of the triangular valley, and fired a good many shots at them. Whenever they attempted to escape we fired a hundred yards in front of them; this raised a cloud of dust, and caused them to turn in another direction. By this means we kept them running in a circle for a considerable time, and shot six out of nine of them.

We were much disappointed at not meeting with any rhinoceri. We kept coming across their *spoor*, and wasted a good deal of time in tracking them. We found this district pretty full of game, and heard of elephants a few miles to the north; this decided us to form camp near Mangive.

The morning after we had shot the gemsbok we were busy preparing the skins with arsenical soap, when a party of Matabele came up and informed us that we had no right to shoot in their country without having the permission of the king. We held an *indaba* (palava), and discussed the matter. Dick was the only one of our party who could converse with them in their own language.

One of my horses had turned out rather a useless beast, and would not stand fire, so we agreed that Dick should return with the *indunas*, procure the needed permission, and make the king a present of the horse.

They started off that day for Gubulawayo, the king's residence. Meanwhile, we spent

MATABELE ASKING FOR OUR RIGHT FOR SHOOTING.

our time in reading, visiting some Matabele kraals, sewing on buttons, etc. I did a little fishing in a tributary of the Shasi River, and caught a few small fish somewhat like our dace. The Matabeles here are called " Makalakas," and are a fine race. The girls especially are very well developed, and wear only a fringe of beads or grass round their waists. They took, as usual, a great interest in our belongings, crowding round us, feeling our clothes, and touching our hands timidly. We did a little useful trading with them for beads and curiosities.

Dick returned at last with permission to shoot, but we were not to go north of Mangwe. This was rather a damper, as the best shooting was that which lay between the king's kraal and the Zambesi. We *trekked* for a few days and formed camp near our boundary without seeing much game, and very few inhabitants. The country was mostly dense bush.

We had just halted at the foot of an open hill, and were lying on the grass, smoking and chatting. One servant was busy unloading things off the wagon; two more were pitching the tent, whilst the "leader" had taken the oxen to the foot of the hill to graze. Leaving them, he had entered the bush for the purpose of making up a bundle of dry wood for the fires.

We were just saying what a likely-looking place it was for lions and other game. As far as the eye could see there stretched a park-like country, with here and there a tract of dense bush. Fine pasture waved over the land, which was intersected by clear flowing streams that rippled into the larger tributaries of the Limpopo.

Suddenly fearful agonizing screams pierced our ears from the bush at the foot of the hill. "By Jove! a lion has got him!" we cried, and seizing our rifles we rushed down; but the yelling had ceased by the time we reached

A MATABELE BELLE.

Q

it, and separating a few yards apart from each other, we entered the bush. We had not gone very far when a shot was fired, and we heard Dick's voice yelling to go to him in all haste. Rushing to the spot, a dreadful sight met our eyes.

The black boy had been picking up sticks under a tree, upon a branch of which a huge boa constrictor lay. The brute had dropped upon him, taken him in his coils to the trunk of the tree, and wound himself round the boy and the tree, crushing him against it. Every bone in his body was broken, sharp ends were sticking through his skin, and his eyeballs were starting out of his head. The expression on his face was awful to look at. The snake had stopped whilst making his final coil, and was glaring at us with open mouth and quivering tongue. We all fired instantly, and fired again ; some shots missed in our haste, but one bullet had shattered the head. A few more finished him. We uncoiled the huge thing, and the unfortunate boy fell, a lifeless pulp of gory flesh and crushed bones, to the ground.

We all felt sick ; it was a sight never to be forgotten, and haunted us for many a day. We never dreamt of meeting a boa in those parts. One had been shot a year or two before in the same country, and I saw the skin hanging in Davis' Boarding-House in Leydenburg, and it measured 17 feet ; this one measured 16 feet.

We buried the boy the same night close to the spot.

The next day we mounted our horses and rode out in quest of lions, as their roaring had kept us awake all through the night. We did not feel much inclined for sport ; the experience of the night before had taken all the heart out of us. We had ridden into some bush, and before emerging into the open space again, took a careful survey through the bushes. It was as well that we did, for we saw

the beautiful sight of a small herd of giraffe
walking slowly along, cropping the tender
shoots of grass and leaves. We each picked
our animal, and fired at 200 yards; two fell to
the ground, vainly striving to rise, throwing
up their long necks in distress; the others
galloped-across the veldt. We gave chase,
and saw that one, very much in the rear,
was labouring in her stride.

We did not succeed in running her down
until we had pursued her for nearly a
mile. Then we all set to work at skin-
ning, and placed some of the meat and
skins in a tree.

There is a great difference between the
flesh of the cow and the bull; that of the
former being excellent, of the latter almost
uneatable. Whilst we were busy at this,
Marston saw a fine bustard, or *pauw*, rise
from the ground and walk away at a distance
of a hundred yards. He made a neat shot,
shooting it through the neck, thus not spoil-

ing any of the flesh, and giving us a handsome addition to our stock-pot.

Shortly after this we saw two lions disappear between a couple of *kopjes* that stood close together, and we made a plan of attack. The elder Marston and I galloped round to the other side to intercept them, whilst Dick and his man rode to where we had seen them disappear. We soon arrived at the spot, and, dismounting, left our horses, and walked down cautiously and quietly through the stunted bushes, expecting every moment to meet the lions. All at once we saw them lying on some flat rocks. I whispered to Marston to fire. He raised his piece, and took what I thought was an absurdly long aim ; before he had pulled the trigger the male had seen us and bounded to his feet. Marston fired then, and missed. The female was lying a little below the male, and as the report rang out, she jumped up and bolted with four little cubs at her heels. The lion stood with lashing tail, as if determined to guard his family. Marston fired again and wounded him mortally, for he fell and lay gasping on the rock. I fired to make sure, and finished him off. Having seen that he lay quite still and apparently dead, we ran down in pursuit of the others, and arrived just in time to see Dick drop the lioness with an easy shot. The little ones were quite old enough to be weaned, but all the same we felt sorry for them, for they all stood in a row next the dead mother, making a purring sound, equivalent, I suppose, to a kitten's mewing. As we advanced, the little beggars put up their backs and snarled most viciously, walking backwards; then they stood close together and watched us skin their mother.

As it was getting dark we rode home, picking up our giraffe meat and skins. We had had a good day, and quite close to the camp too.

We stayed here for a fortnight, and shot over the country for miles round — lions, giraffes, koodoos, hartebeeste, wildebeeste, rhinoceri, and many other game. Hearing of some buffalo about twenty miles to the east, we *trekked* in that direction in search of some sport with them : a few elephants were also reported to be about there.

Two of us generally rode in front of the wagon, getting an occasional shot at something. One morning the Marstons were riding about half a mile in front, when one of them came galloping back, saying that they had distinctly heard the trumpeting of an elephant at no great distance. We seized our elephant rifles and rode in the direction from whence the sound had come. Fortunately, the wind was in our favour, and at last, after two hours' search, we caught sight of them.

There were seven in all, somewhat scattered, so we separated and dodged them through the bush. I soon got a chance at a fine bull, with a handsome pair of tusks, and fired. At the same moment the Marstons fired : we had all wounded our beasts, and gave chase. It was no easy matter to work our way through the thick bush, and I could hear several shots fired by the others, who had made better progress than I. It proved lucky that they had done so, for five of the elephants doubled back, and I saw them coming straight towards me. Dismounting next a large tree, I waited for a few minutes, and as they passed I fired at the ear of a cow, with long thin tusks, and killed her with one shot. Before I could reload, the next one had passed. The third one proved to be the wounded bull who had my 4-oz. bullet lodged in his forearm. At the same time, he managed to go at a good pace. He was making straight for the tree where I was standing ready for him.

At this moment my steady old horse stepped forward to crop some grass near my feet, and I was obliged to bend down to take his bridle to back him as quickly as possible. At that instant the old elephant saw me.

Extending his huge ears, he charged, screaming with rage, a very different sound indeed to the usual trumpeting. I waited until he got within fifteen yards, and fired full at his chest, and dodged back behind the tree. He gave a kind of trumpet and staggered past me, and then stood swaying a little. I did not wait to reload, but taking my 577 bore from my servant, let fire at his ear-hole, and the great beast dropped into a kneeling posture, quite dead. I had heard a good many shots fired by the others, and sent my servant to look for them and report results, whilst I took a rest, seated upon the leg of the dead cow. The Marstons soon came up, and said they had dropped two; one had not been killed until ten large bullets had been put into him; the other was finished with two 577. From our own experience, and from what we heard from other sportsmen, a small bore, say 450 or 577, with a hardened bullet, is much more reliable than the heavy 4-oz. bore, besides being less dangerous and giving less pain to the poor brutes, which precaution, I regret to say, is little heeded by a number of so-called great hunters. To illustrate this, I will only quote the words of the late Gordon Cumming :—

" Having planted a bullet in the shoulder bone of an elephant, and caused the agonized creature to lean for support against a tree, I proceeded to brew some coffee. Having refreshed myself, taking observations of the elephant's spasms and writhings between the sips, I resolved to make experiments on vulnerable points, and approaching very near, I fired several bullets at different parts of his enormous skull. He only acknowledged the shots by a salaam-like movement of his trunk, with the point of which he gently touched the wounds with a striking and peculiar action. Surprised and shocked to find that I was only prolonging the suffering of the noble beast, which bore its trials with such dignified composure, I resolved to finish the proceeding with all possible despatch, and accordingly opened fire upon him from the left side. Aiming at the shoulder, I fired six shots with the two-grooved rifle, which must have eventually proved mortal, after which I fired six shots at the same part with the Dutch six - pounder. Large tears now trickled down from his eyes, which he slowly shut and opened, his colossal frame shivered convulsively, and falling on his side he expired."

All this is inexcusable, as over and over again Mr Cumming relates how he slew this and that giant beast with a single well-directed shot.

We sent for axes, and soon chopped out the tusks, which altogether weighed 250 lbs., some steaks off the youngest animal, and a foot, which we had heard was very good eating. We cooked the foot South African fashion, which is by making a hole in the ground about the size of the foot, then making a large fire in and over the hole. When the fire has settled down to a red glow, it is all pulled out and the foot put in. Over the foot a few inches of earth are laid, and a large fire is then built on top, and in two hours it is ready for eating, the skin being easily cut through with a knife. We found it very tender and glutinous, but not much flavour.

A day or two after our sport with the elephants we sighted a herd of buffalo, and rode out, skirting a tract of dense bush which bordered the plain, and thus getting close enough for a shot. As before, we picked our animals and fired together.

One fell dead from Dick's rifle, and we mounted and gave chase after the rest. We had not gone far when the herd suddenly stopped, and huddling up together, as they generally do, stared at us. Scrambling off, we fired again at 200 yards, and another fell bellowing to the ground, rose, and fell again. Dick stopped to despatch this fellow, while we chased the rest, but only succeeded in obtaining one more, which one of us had wounded. I saw it charge Marston, who bolted a few yards, and climbed up a small tree. Knowing that it would charge me, I rode towards another tree in case of danger, but decided to stand underneath it and dodge the brute, so as to have a better chance of killing it. The buffalo, sighting me, came charging on, and I fired at fifteen paces, and sprang to one side. Before he could charge again, I shot him through the heart, just as he was turning.

We were a mile away from where we had left Dick, and wondered why he had not come on. There was a rise in the ground between him and us, and when we arrived on the top of this we could see his horse grazing, but no sign of him. Riding hastily on, we discovered poor old Dick lying gasping under the body of the dead buffalo. Our servants were running towards us from the bush, and with our combined efforts we rolled the beast off. We found the poor fellow terribly mutilated, gored through the body, also with an arm broken. There was nothing to be done, and he died a few minutes afterwards.

We buried him that evening at the same spot. His brother was terribly grieved, and sat up all night on a box, with his face in his hands, sometimes rocking himself to and fro.

Everyone liked Dick : he was a thorough sportsman, and always a jolly companion.

The winter was drawing to a close, and this sad event happening, we decided to return, and told the boys so, who were delighted at the prospect of getting away from the lions.

We did not return by the route we intended to, as we found it was infested with the *tetse-*fly, besides being a longer way round. We had had fairly good sport, considering the time we were hunting, as the pile of skins and horns in the wagon could testify.

Instead of going to Pietermaritzburg, we travelled to Kimberley, where we sold every-thing except the skins and horns, which Marston took to England with him, expect-ing to get better prices than we were offered, which he did, as I saw by the cheque he sent me.

CHAPTER XII.

I FELT very lonely in Kimberley, not knowing a soul, and missed my chum Dick, with whom I had spent years of ups and downs.

As a place of residence, Kimberley is one of the most unpleasant I have ever been in.

It is situated in the centre of some vast Karroo plains, with not a tree or even a hill in sight, and no river within fifteen miles.

Being a drought-stricken place, it is frequently plagued with red dust storms, which come rolling over the veldt, smothering everything in the town. There are four mines situated within two miles of each other —Kimberley, De Beers, Du Toitspan and

R

Bultfontein. When they were first discovered in 1870, the diamonds were found
in yellow earth, and thousands flocked from
all parts, and pegged out their claims.

This yellow ground was worked to a depth
of about 50 feet, when they came upon hard
blue ground. Thinking they had arrived at
"bottom," many abandoned their claims,
others sold out at a trifle, which afterwards
fetched upwards of £12,000 each, when it
was found that this blue ground was the true
diamondiferous soil, and went down to unknown depths. Companies were now floated,
machinery erected, and in a few years a town
of 25,000 inhabitants flourished on these arid
plains.

"Stages" were built on the edge of the
mine, on which were fixed huge "hoppers,"
into which the blue ground was tipped from
large buckets holding over a ton, which were
drawn up on wire ropes, attached to "drums"
on the engines placed behind the stages.

As the drum revolves it draws one bucket up, at the same time letting an empty one down. Trucks pass under these hoppers, and are rapidly drawn away on rails by horses to the depositing floors. These floors extend for acres, and the "blue," which contains a quantity of lime, cover the floors, and, after hosing, it partly crumbles with the action of air and water. Gangs of natives are employed, who walk along in lines crushing the "blue" with the flat side of picks. Other trucks come after them, taking the pulverised soil to the washing machine. There it is hoisted by elevators, and falls into the puddling cylinder, into which there is a steady flow of water, and the revolving arms and teeth turn it into thin mud. The diamonds and other heavy matter rest on the bottom, while the lighter material flows down a "shoot" into the "tailing pit," from whence another elevator lifts it into a high shoot, and it finally settles in a huge mound some distance away. The heavy deposit in the pan is cleaned out every twelve hours, and put through a machine called a "pulsator," which further concentrates it; thus 240 loads of earth are reduced to one load of gravel to be sorted. The sorting is done on tables, first wet by white men, then dry by natives.

The largest diamond found in these four mines weighed $42\frac{1}{2}$ carats, but afterwards one was found at Jagersfontein weighing $969\frac{1}{2}$ carats. Notwithstanding the vigilance of the detective department, it is calculated that upwards of half a million sterling value of diamonds are stolen annually.

Every gang of natives working in the mine or on the floors is watched by the overseers, and every now and then searched by a "searcher." Even so, they manage either to secrete them on their bodies, or swallow them. This done, they generally leave their employers, sell the diamond or diamonds to an illicit diamond buyer (I.D.B.), and leave the fields, or obtain employment elsewhere. They are obliged to leave their situation to enable them to find a buyer, as all the natives employed are compelled to live in compounds. These consist of rows of galvanised iron buildings forming a square, enclosed by a high fence. Here there are shops where they can purchase all they require ; swimming-baths, hospital, and wood and water are provided free. They are compelled to remain prisoners, as it were, in this area until their three months' engagement has expired, at the end of which time many of them re-engage for further periods. They are strictly guarded against outer communication, and are searched on leaving the mine on their way to the compound. There are several entrances to the mines which are guarded night and day by officers of the Searching Department, which was in my time connected with the Detective Department. I applied for an appointment to this

Department, hearing that the officers were gentlemen, and exceedingly well paid. My references were referred to and found satisfactory, and, after a month's idleness, I was appointed searching officer in the Bultfontein mine.

I forgot to mention that Philip Marston, who was a wealthy man, declined to take Dick's share of money lying in the bank at Leydenburg.

In the two years I spent in the mines and drafted from one to the other, I saw many chances of investing money profitably, and had accumulated a large balance at my bank, and one day, giving notice to my chief, I booked as passenger by the mail for England.

COMMISSIONER STREET, JOHANNESBURG.

CHAPTER XIII.

SINCE my departure from South Africa, two important changes have occurred, namely the Witwatersrand Gold-Fields, and the British Chartered Company of South Africa. Before the discovery of the former, the gold-fields of South Africa were certainly not much attraction. The first to find gold at the Rand was a Mr Struben, who spent £11,000 on the spot before getting any return. Many companies were soon afterwards floated, and the output in September 1895 was 194,764 oz.

The town of Johannesburg, situated 5,735 feet above the sea, is on the Rand, and the land falls suddenly to the north so quickly that Pretoria, which is only thirty-five miles off, is 1,600 feet lower. This height gives Johannesburg a fine climate, and makes it cold, if not the coldest town in South Africa.

A few years ago there was not a tree to be seen, but owing to the richness of the soil, not only do large trees now flourish, but rows of green hedges fringe fields and gardens, recalling our English lanes. The town is becoming the largest city in South Africa. It is not a beautiful town, but handsome buildings are being erected, the streets improved and lighted with electric light, and there are three miles of tramway.

Railway communication extends to the Cape 1014 miles, to Delagoa Bay 395 miles, and to Durban about 438 miles.

As far as gold is concerned, South Africa is practically a reef country, no alluvial deposits of any extent having been found. But that is not to say they will not be discovered. No country in the world has better prospects than it has, and the fortunes of many lie hidden, waiting to be unearthed.

Some fields show their gold in massive belts of quartz running vertically or horizontally (called floating), others in thin veins between

slate and shales, while, at the Rand, the gold is
found in a hard conglomerate called "banket,"
which runs in a form of reef, covers hundreds of
square miles of country, and sinks to unknown
depths ; in other words, it is inexhaustible.

It is hardly worth while giving a detailed
description of gold extraction, as most would
be bored with such, while a short account may
interest many and be skipped by the others.

The work first commenced by digging
trenches and sinking shafts with the dip of
the reef. This system was then done away
with, and vertical shafts fitted with "skips"
were sunk, cutting the parallel reefs. As the
shaft descends, levels are made into the reef ;
the ore is then hoisted up through these shafts
by machinery and taken to the batteries,
where it is first broken into pieces the
size of lump sugar, and then put into the
mortar box. Five heavy stamps, each falling
with the weight of nearly a thousand pounds,
drop into a mortar box and form a battery.
Some mills have considerably more than a

hundred stamps. Each stamp falls ninety times a minute, and the noise of a large number at work, crushing the ore to powder, is almost deafening.

The ore crushed, the wet pulp is run over copper plate-tables on which mercury is laid, with which the gold alone amalgamates ; from this it runs through mercury troughs, thence over blankets laid in other troughs, which catch all the remaining gold. The tailings run on into mounds or pits for further treatment by the cyanide process, which extracts the silver and the remaining gold. Now and then the batteries are stopped, and the amalgam is cleaned up and put into a retort, which is placed into a furnace. The heat causes the mercury to vaporise, and it is caught by the condenser and reliquefied and bottled for further use. The gold left in the retort is melted in crucibles and poured into moulds.

Johannesburg has already more European advantages than any other city in South Africa. Fine hotels, clubs, shops with Parisian and

London wares, theatres, polo clubs, rinks, and whatever reckless expenditure can procure in the way of comfort and distraction is to be had there. The value of building sites has increased enormously, and one hears of £40,000 being paid for a "stand" that was bought for a few hundreds six years ago. Commodities are getting cheaper with the railway and increased facilities for traffic.

Some day, no doubt, it will be the seat of a fierce struggle between the British population, assisted by the foreigner—French, German, or Spanish, as the case may be—against the "want-wit," blind policy, and petty tyranny of the Boer official.

It is to the interest of the capitalist to keep matters going smoothly, but the rapidly increasing British population, with families growing up around them to cement their interest, all tax-paying members of the community, must eventually predominate ; the dissatisfaction will one day bubble over and find outlet in a Transvaal war.

CHAPTER XIV.

WITH regard to the British Chartered Company, little need be said, as it is so well known. The great capabilities of the country which they lay claim to are, in my opinion, not exaggerated in the least. What I saw of their vast dominions impressed me that a great future was before it. They own and have mineral rights over a tract of country larger than France, Germany, Austria, and Italy combined—a country rich in minerals, probably precious stones, and some of the finest grazing and agricultural land in the world. Over a hundred payable reefs have been found, and the country is advancing with rapid strides. Half a dozen newspapers are published, railway, telegraph, and postal communication established, towns springing up like mushrooms, and many people flocking there, confident of making a "pile" one way or another. Land can be purchased in Mashonaland at 9d. an acre, in Matabeleland at 1s. 6d. per acre, both subject to conditions.

People going there are chiefly interested in mining, little farming having been commenced; but there is no doubt as to whether it would pay or not with land at that price, and fancy prices to be obtained for produce. An acquaintance of mine there made several thousands by growing vegetables alone, profits sometimes amounting to £150 a month. This may seem an exaggeration, but when a few acres of cabbages at half a crown each, onions at sixpence, and other vegetables at like prices are reckoned up, it is probable enough.

The all-round man is the best man for the

Colony, and any youngster with a decent education, not afraid of hard work, with a pair of hands fit for practical use, who can ride and work hard, will make his way there. A little knowledge of carpentering or forge work is worth more than all the Latin and Greek crammed in college to a fellow trying to make his way in South Africa. It is a great country with a great future, and there is space and to spare for intelligent men.

THE END.

www.ingramcontent.com/pod-product-compliance
Lightning Source LLC
Chambersburg PA
CBHW021058030726
47496CB00006B/1895

* 9 7 8 3 7 4 4 7 5 1 6 5 0 *